FUELED BY FIRE

2020 FICTION FANTASTIC YOUNG WRITERS SHORT FICTION CONTEST

FUELED BY FIRE
The 2020 Fiction Fantastic Young Writers Short Fiction Contest

Wordcrafters in Eugene
425 Lincoln Street
Eugene, OR 97401
www.wordcrafters.org

ISBN: 978-1-64388-443-1

Wordcrafters in Eugene

Staff

Daryll Lynne Evans, Executive Director

Jorah LaFleur, WITS Director

Leah Velez, Curriculum and Content Coordinator

Jenni Larson, Intern

Prenapa Techakumthon, Intern

Fiction Fantastic Contest Coordinator

Drea Lee

Board of Directors

Nina Hofmeijer, President

Patricia Marshall, Past President

Christina Lay

Matt Lowes

Drea Lee

Anthology Staff

Editors: Daryll Lynne Evans and Leah Velez
Design: Luminare Press

Writers in the Schools

Writers-in-Residence

Jorah LaFleur

Carter McKenzie

Participating Classroom Teachers

Shannon Hart, Elmira High School

Kris Olsen, Kalapuya High School

Stephan Willow, John Serbu Youth Campus

Fiction Fantastic Judge

J.C. Geiger

Writers in the Schools is a program of Wordcrafters in Eugene, a non-profit literary organization whose mission is to provide writers and readers opportunities to strengthen their craft, deepen their connection with literature, and share their knowledge with each other and with future generations.

For more information please contact:

Wordcrafters in Eugene
425 Lincoln Street
Eugene, OR 97401
www.wordcrafters.org

Sponsors

Bloomfield Family Foundation

Braemar Charitable Trust

City of Eugene

Cow Creek Umpqua Indian Foundation

Elizabeth George Foundation

Harvest Foundation

Herbert A. Templeton Foundation

Lane Arts Council

Luminare Press

MillsDavis Foundation

Oregon Country Fair

Oregon Arts Commission

Oregon Community Foundation

Shkspr.Designs

Spirit Mountain Community Fund

Teach Write Now

Individual Donors

Stacy Allen
Evelyn Anderton
Joanna Bartlett
Belly Vision LLC
Ben Brock
Terry Brooks
Valerie Brooks
Bill Cameron
Liane Cordes
Al and Liz Cratty
Kay Crider
Anne Dean
Vicki Elmer
Daryll Lynne Evans
Sarah Finlay
Val Ford
Elizabeth George
Henry Goswick
Lynda Green
Louann Guzman
Talia Hagen
Michael Harris
Julie Hessler
Kim Hunter
Denise Jessup
Kali Kardas
Elise Kimmons
Alexis Lanham
Christina Lay
Stephanie LeMenager
Matt Lowes
Dana Magliari
Jean Manor
George Filgate and
Patricia Marshall
M.K. Martin
Debra Meadow
Juanita Metzler
Jamie and Michael
Moffit
Lise Nelson
Kevin O'Brien
Carla Orcutt
Kari and Craig Parsons
Caralee and Fred Roberts
Ellen Saunders
Jenny Schrader
Dev Sinha
Lexis Sixel
Kellie Skrepetos
Morgan Songi
Karen Stillwagon
Tex Thompson
The Walkers
Eric Witchey
Leah Velez

Contents

Wayward Blazes

Rising from the Ashes

Introduction

"Because giving people stories is not a luxury. It's actually one of the things that you live and die for."

—Neil Gaiman

The world has changed drastically from the beginning of February 2020 when students first submitted their stories to one that feels like a sci-fi movie gone awry: Global pandemic! Quarantine! Murder hornets! With school cancelled, along with sports, birthday parties, and anything that brings us within six feet of each other, social distancing has touched almost every aspect of our lives.

What we have turned to—whether in film or show or book or graphic novel form—are stories.

In the stories that fill these pages, young writers demonstrate the very properties that make literature one of the most essential tools to help us understand the world. From their tales, we learn to find hope amid difficulties and despair, adventures to slip into to escape our worries, and moments of connection and discovery that help us navigate these challenging times.

Fiction Fantastic is one of the few opportunities in Lane County to showcase student writing or provide creative writing instruction. In our seventh year of the contest in 2020, 145 entries poured in from across Lane County, young writers took part in creative writing workshops and write-ins, teachers loved the engaging curriculum (and stickers!) we developed to help bring creative writing to their classrooms, and—thanks to Luminare Press—young writers get to see their words in print in the Winners Anthology!

The selection process is highly competitive for Fiction Fantastic. First, stories go through two rounds of blind judging, read by a panel of twenty-three volunteer judges made up of writers, educators, and community members. Then the top stories in each grade grouping go to our celebrity judge (still without identifying student info), who selects the winning stories and placements. Finalists learn their placement at the Fiction Fantastic awards ceremony, where they also get to share a short reading from their work.

We cannot do this work without the tremendous support of our community of writers, educators, volunteers, and parents, not to mention the many foundations and local businesses that support our youth programs. (And a special shout out to our volunteer Fiction Fantastic Contest Coordinator, Drea Lee, who managed every aspect of the contest with finesse and grace.)

Fiction Fantastic is a part of our Writers in the Schools programs for young writers. Wordcrafters in Eugene has built a strong foundation for our Writers in the Schools (WITS) program. Since its launch, the WITS program has served over 4900 students across Lane County, including schools in rural and under-served areas.

Most notably for the 2019-2020 school year (and in spite of the school year being cut short), we held five writer residencies: two in Kalapuya High School, two in the Phoenix Program at John Serbu Youth Campus, and a pilot residency at Elmira High School.

All WITS programs strive to give young writers a space to tell their stories. Our goal is to empower students to find their voice and understand their voice is powerful. Writing is of course important, but that is only the first step.

What we see time and again in WITS is how vital it is to

create a space for young writers to share their stories with each other and with the world. Whether it's the seniors at Elmira High School reading their spoken word poems aloud on stage, or students at Kalapuya High School seeing their words in print, or the students of the Phoenix Program at Serbu Youth Campus creating multi-media spoken word videos, or the young writers who enter Fiction Fantastic and see their work published in the anthology, when students have the opportunity to share their work and hear the response, they finally understand the power of their voice and their stories.

We hope you enjoy this year's Winners Anthology, featuring twelve talented writers. We love how these stories transport us to strange new worlds and immerse us deep into the psyches of characters discovering who they are.

This anthology illustrates the power and importance of literature, particularly in trying times. Join us as we continue to nurture our young writers and future storytellers so that they, in turn, can tell the stories of hope, connection, and endurance we need to face the challenges life presents us. Read on!

Sincerely,

Daryll Lynne Evans, Executive Director,
Wordcrafters in Eugene

About Fiction Fantastic Judge J. C. Geiger

J. C. Geiger has eaten the beating heart of a snake, been deported from a full-moon party, and spent a short time locked in a Bolivian prison. He also writes fiction. His short works have appeared in the pages of Murky Depths and Horror Garage, and on stage at The Second City in Chicago. His debut novel, *Wildman*, (Little, Brown Books for Young Readers) earned the Kirkus Star, was named as a Top YA Book of 2017 by Amazon editors, and was featured by Banks Street as one of The Best Children's Books of the Year.

2020 Fiction Fantastic Winners

Elementary School (Grades 3-5)

First Place: Monroe Colbath, "The Camping Trip"
Elmira Elementary School

Second Place: Allie Nichols, "Portal"
Douglas Gardens Elementary School

Third Place: Rogue Miles-Waybrant, "The Dream"
Gilham Elementary School

Honorable Mention: Abbigail Park, "Stinkmutt and Trashcat"
River Road/El Camino del Río Elementary School

Middle School

First Place: Peyton Tyner, "The No Named Soldier"
Eugene Christian School

Second Place: Emily Krauss, "Disappearing Act"
Pleasant Hill Middle School

Third Place: Ava Thompson, "The Story of Magissa Stry"
Kennedy Middle School

Honorable Mention: Brianna Bird, "Heart of Ice"
Eugene Christian School

High School

First Place: Natasha Dracobly, "Skyline"
South Eugene High School

Second Place: Gracie Bratland, "A Dualistic Dichotomy"
Churchill High School

Third Place: Emma Martins, "The Fading Friend"
Willamette High School

Honorable Mention: Elizabeth Meigs, "Clones"
Marist High School

Honorable Mention: Natasha Dracobly, "When the Sun Goes Down"
South Eugene High School

Strike the Flint

The Story of Magissa Stry

By Ava Thompson

Kennedy Middle School

Chapter 1

I didn't mean to catch Mrs. Pyrah on fire. I really didn't. Honestly, it's her fault.

"Maj-EE-sa, please turn to the correct page!" Mrs. Pyrah said in her nasally voice.

"I AM on the correct page, and I told you my name is pronounced Ma-gis-a!!" I said.

Mrs. Pyrah frowned and angrily said, "Don't you give me attitude, young lady, you're disrupting the class!"

"No," I said, "now YOU'RE disrupting class."

Her face briefly flashed angrily, then it was deadly calm.

"Uh, oh," I thought to myself.

"I knew you would be trouble as soon as I heard about your father," she said with an evil smile.

"She wouldn't!" I thought.

Mrs. Pyrah had the class's full attention now. She wouldn't tell about my father for real, would she? I mean, I knew she had it out for me, but this? This was truly evil.

"So, Maj-EE-sa."

Oh, no, here it comes.

"How long has your father been locked up in St. Parafron?"

Everyone knew now. St. Parafron was widely known as the biggest insane asylum on Mikro Planiti. Everyone's attention was now on me. They all stared at me as if I had a giant griffin on my head, only in a bad way. A couple of the kids twisted their faces in disgust, others looked confused, some of them smirked.

One yelled out, "The apple doesn't fall far from the tree!"

Everyone in the class laughed, but the person laughing the hardest was none other than Mrs. Pyrah herself. In fact, instead of punishing the boy, she came and rewarded him with candy! I was so angry, not only had she singled me out, but she had rewarded the kid who had insulted me! All these things that teachers are never supposed to do. I could feel my face getting hot as I gritted my teeth and reminded myself that if I did anything, I would get in trouble. I stared so hard at Mrs. Pyrah I thought she would catch on fire.

And then to my—and everyone else's—surprise, she did! She started screaming and yelling! Then she turned and looked at me and screamed, "YOU DID THIS!!!! YOU . . . ARE A WITCH!!!!"

"No, it wasn't me! I swear!" I said, panicking. I wondered though, could I?

"WITCH! WITCH! WITCH!" chanted the class. I felt my stomach drop.

Mrs. Pyrah finally doused herself with water and promptly fainted! Oh, I was in trouble now. Some people in the class started walking towards me, arms outstretched as if to grab a hold of me.

"Get the witch!" some yelled.

A burst of fear and adrenaline shot through me. I took a quick look around the room and saw an open window. I ran and jumped out the window. I landed weird and felt my ankle twist. I let out a small strangled squeal as I felt a sharp pain in my ankle. I heard a thump behind me and whipped around to see the boy who had made fun of me, he looked angry and scared, as if I scared him and infuriated him at the same time. Fake it 'til you make it, I thought.

"Stand back!" I said with fake confidence and my hand outstretched.

He stopped and a look of fear came across his face.

"Turn around!" I said.

When he didn't, I threateningly pointed my hand at him. At that he quickly turned around and faced the school. I made sure he wasn't looking, and when I saw he wasn't, I turned and ran as fast as my injured ankle would allow. As I ran I winced as my ankle throbbed. I turned down my street and told myself, just a little further. I burst through the door of my house, panting and on the verge of tears. I ran to the kitchen and collapsed.

"Are you okay, honey?" The voice of my mother cut through my thoughts.

I breathlessly told her the whole story. She thought for a moment with her brow furrowed, then she jumped up and started running around the house gathering up little things and shoving them in a backpack she pulled from a cupboard.

"What are you doing?" I asked

She replied with, "No time to explain!"

With that, she went over to the wall and pressed on it. I was confused until I saw that it opened a small compartment. And she said into it, "*Anoixe!*"

The wall opened up to reveal dozens of scrolls, bottles of strange liquids, and jars of what looked like dried animal parts! My mother quickly started shoving things in the pack.

"Mom," I said. "What is going on? What are you doing?"

Instead of answering my question, she simply shoved a bottle of gold liquid in my hand and said urgently, "This is for your ankle." When I hesitated, she said, "Hurry, we don't have much time!"

At that, I quickly downed the contents of the bottle. It tasted like honey and somehow like sunshine, then I felt the dull throb of my ankle subside.

"What is this stuff?" I asked in wonder.

"Healing potion," my mother replied.

"Did you say healing potion!?!?" I said, thinking I hadn't heard her right.

"No, I said apple juice. Yes, I said healing potion!" my mother said sarcastically.

She then shoved one last scroll in the satchel and thrust it into my hand. She kissed me on the forehead and said, "Just remember that I will always love you, no matter what happens." As she said this, I saw tears in her eyes.

"Now I need you to get out of here as soon as you can."

"Where am I gonna go?" I said with a lump in my throat.

"Anywhere but here, now go!" she replied motioning me out the door.

"Bye, Mom. I love you," I said as my throat got tight, and I felt a single tear make its way down my face.

"I love you, too, Maggie," she said, using my old nickname.

Then I quickly went to the door and looked back to take one last look around my home, stopping on my mother's face. She smiled sadly and waved goodbye. I waved back, and then I turned and ran out the door.

Chapter 2

The forest was pitch black in the dim light of dusk, I could barely see my own feet. As I ran, I stumbled over root after root until finally I couldn't hear anything, and I stopped to catch my breath. I sat against a tree to see if there was anything of use in the backpack my mother had given me. I reached into the bag and found a strange yellow ball labeled, "Shake me." "What else do I have to lose?" I thought and gave the yellow ball a good hard shake. To my surprise, the ball started to float and glow brightly. I smiled and gently moved it so I could get a proper look in the bag. Inside I rummaged around until I found a letter labeled "To my dearest Maggie" in my mother's handwriting. I felt a lump in my throat as I tore open the seal of the letter and began to read:

Dear Maggie,

I wish that I could have stopped this, I wanted to tell you that you were magic, but I could never find the perfect moment. I know you think that you are the reason for your father's sanity slipping away, and I can understand that, but it is not true in the slightest. When I told him you had inherited your great grandmother's gift, I hadn't thought that he would go running to the police. He wasn't crazy at first. It was just when no one believed him that he started to obsess. I remember one evening, I came home and you were crying at the kitchen table and your father was repeatedly saying, "Tell me the truth!" You, of course, had no idea what he was talking about, so you were very frightened. That was the day I decided it was best if you went to public school with all the other children instead of staying home with your father. Anyway, I'm getting off topic, in the satchel

you will find these things and much more: (By the way this satchel is bigger on the inside)
This letter (obviously)

A light ball
Healing potion
Dried fish, cheese, bread, and a flask of water
Small potion book
A blanket
An expandable tent
A tarp
And my love

I wish you well in whatever fate throws at you. I love you, Maggie.

Sincerely, Mom

A tear traced its way down my face and landed on the letter, leaving a small wet blotch on the slightly yellowed parchment. I let myself sit and wallow in my own sorrow for a moment longer, and then I wiped my tears away and got up. “Let’s see that tent,” I said to myself. I dug in the backpack and felt around. I hadn’t realized it before, but the bag was really deep! After a couple minutes of digging around and coming up with a host of strange potion ingredients, I finally pulled my hand out of the pack and, low and behold, the tent! I walked around a bit to see if I could find a nice flat spot to set up, doing so proved to be difficult due to the fact that I was in full growth forest full of roots. In addition to that, my long wily auburn hair kept getting tangled up in tree branches and thorns, so I had to keep stopping and untangling myself.

As if things couldn't get any worse, I heard a roll of thunder, and it started pouring rain. Finally I found a clearing and set up the tent. I grimaced at the size of the tent, seeing that it was the size of a doghouse. Sighing, I lifted the tent flap and looked inside. I was shocked to see that the inside of the tent was the size of the average bedroom! I smiled and laughed to myself in amazement. I don't remember much after that, I remember pulling a sleeping bag out of the pack in a haze and falling in to a deep, blissful sleep.

Chapter 3

I woke up to find that several animals had gotten into my tent and were sleeping on top of me, one of which was a midnight black cat with electric green eyes, which were a stunning contrast to my chocolate brown eyes. Once I had shooed all the animals out, I saw that the cat was still there. I sighed,

"What do you want, cat?" I snapped.

"Nothing," replied the cat in a strange British accent.

I jumped back in surprise.

"D-did you just talk?" I stuttered.

"What does it sound like?" the cat said, sarcastically rolling its eyes.

"Okay," I said, thinking out loud. "I'm in the middle of the woods with a talking cat, and I'm running away. Man, never thought that would happen."

"You need some help," the cat stated matter-of-factly.

"Says the talking cat," I replied.

I sat down and started to eat some of the bread I had found in my bag. When I spotted the cat eyeing it with a hungry look, I sighed and threw him a chunk of bread.

"Well, I never!" the cat exclaimed.

"What?" I asked alarmed.

"I cannot possibly eat that bread," he said in disgust. "It's contaminated!"

"Oh, really?" I said.

"I always mean what I say," he replied with his nose turned up.

At that I promptly picked up the piece of bread and popped it in my mouth.

"You filthy beast!" the cat exclaimed in disgust.

"Well, then," I said scowling, "none for you."

"Humph!" the cat huffed.

After I had eaten, I went to pack up and found the cat curled up in my backpack. After numerous attempts to move the cat, I gave up and just packed around him. As I slung the pack onto my shoulder, I grunted under the extra weight but managed not to lose my balance. And with that, I set off.

It was a long day of hiking through the dense brush and crawling under dead logs and jumping over streams. At about midday I stopped in a nice sunny clearing to take a drink of water and eat a little. As I slung the pack off of my back and dropped it on the ground next to me, a muffled "OW!" came from it. I sighed as the cat stumbled out and began to wash his fur.

"How very disrespectful!" the cat exclaimed.

"Says the cat that made me carry him ALL the way here," I replied.

"You don't have to say *cat* like a bad thing," he mumbled grumpily.

"Well, what am I supposed to call you then!" I said exasperated.

"You may call me Midnight," the cat said simply.

"Huh," I said, "nice name."

"I know," Midnight said smiling. "Aren't I amazing?"

"And humble, too," I replied, rolling my eyes.

Just then, one of the bushes near me rustled slightly.

"What the—" was all I had time to say before a man jumped out of the bush and tackled me! With a gasp of astonishment, I realized, that man was my father!

Chapter 4

"D-dad?" I stuttered.

"Don't call me that!" my father rasped.

"W-what are you doing here?" I asked, still stuttering.

"You don't need to know that information," he said menacingly.

Out of the corner of my eye, I saw Midnight disappear into the forest. What a coward, I thought.

"Hey, can you please get off of me so I can hug you?" I asked.

At that, he laughed and laughed.

"Why would I want to hug you?" he replied.

"Well," I said, confused, "I'm your daughter and—"

He cut me off. "You," he growled, "are no daughter of mine!"

And with that, he hit me on the head and everything went black.

I woke up to find myself chained to a wall in a dark room with a barred door. I felt a lump the size of half an egg on my forehead that was throbbing with a painful, steady pulse. I felt dizzy and I couldn't think straight.

I called out hoarsely, "Hello? Is anyone there?"

"Be quiet, witch!" a gruff voice hollered back.

I tested the chains by pulling on them, only to find that they were anchored deep in the wall. I sat there and wondered what they were going to do to me, bury me alive maybe? Burn me at the stake?

A loud clang from outside interrupted my thoughts of death and suffering.

"Hello?" I said tentatively. "Mean man, is that you?"

Without a word my father's evil grin appeared at the bars.

"I knew you were a witch all along!" he said, his face screwing up in disgust.

"No," I said, my smile going all goofy. "You only knew when mom told you, and then you completely broke her trust and betrayed her."

"Well, I, I uh," he stuttered. I could tell through the fog that was my mind that I had hit a sore spot. "It doesn't matter, everyone knows now that you're a witch! They let me go because they realized I'm not crazy!" he said with a hysterical laugh.

"You sound pretty crazy to me," I said smiling.

"Enough of that!" he exclaimed. "You're going to be executed, and there's nothing you can do about it!" And then he walked away laughing.

I felt a tear trace its way down my face as I thought about how I would never see my mother again.

"Finally," said a female voice from the corner. "I thought he'd never leave."

"W-who's there?" I whispered.

A girl materialized in the corner. She had curly blonde hair pulled back in a fashionable pony tail. Her electric blue eyes twinkled as she smiled and said, "C'mon, let's go."

I had butterflies in my stomach as I looked at her.

"You're pretty," slipped out of my mouth before I could stop myself.

"Thanks," she said, her smile becoming even bigger.

"You're welcome," I said, my heart in my throat.

"Oooh," she said reaching out to touch my forehead. "You don't look so good."

I giggled. "Ha, yeah, being kidnapped and taken to jail does that."

She laughed a small puff of a laugh. "Yeah."

"Hey," I said, "what's your name?"

"Me? I'm Sofi."

"I'm Magissa. It's nice to meet you, I'd shake your hand, but I'm chained to the wall."

"Speaking of which, let's fix that," she replied, smiling.

At that she took a bottle of metallic liquid out of a pouch on a belt around her waist. She walked over and took my arm in her hand. I blushed and felt butterflies in my stomach. Why did I feel this way? She poured the liquid on the chain, and I was astonished when the chains melted! She did the same to the other wrist.

"Who are you?" I asked in wonder.

"I'm Sofi Torres, part of the witch rescue team," she replied.

"What's that?" I asked.

"It's part of the W.I.S—Witches in Secret. I'm going to take you there."

"Oh," I said, "thank you."

"No problem." She smiled.

Fast forward three days in the future, we came to an old building.

"Are you ready for this?" Sofi asked, taking my hand.

I glanced down at my hand in hers. "As ready as I'll ever be." She squeezed my hand reassuringly.

"*Anoixe!*" she said to the door.

"Hey, what does that mean?" I asked.

"It means 'open' in Greek, why?" she replied.

"My mom used it to open a cupboard full of potion ingredients!" I exclaimed.

"Huh," she said. "Well, Magissa, welcome to W.I.S!!!!"

The Dream

By Rogue Miles-Waybrant

Gilham Elementary School

1997

The sounds of breathing echoed through the dark forest. There was so much fog I couldn't see anything more than a yard away from me. I pulled my dirt-stained flannel off and wrapped it around my waist. I heard whistling in the distance. I started to get nervous. My eyes darted everywhere there might have been a sound. The wind seemed to whisper into my ear. Suddenly, a silhouetted figure appeared in the fog. I had the urge to ask who was there, but I was too scared. I didn't know why. I decided I didn't have a choice. I had to declare who this mysterious subject was. "Hello?! Is anyone there?" The figure started to get closer. "Only you," the figure said. "What?" I asked, sweat running down my face. "Only you," the figure repeated. "What's happening?!" I yelled, trying to get a clear answer from him. "Only you," the figure repeated. "Stop saying that! I need a real answer from you!" I said, annoyed and scared now. The figure was still saying, "Only you. Only you. Only you." Darkness crowded around me as if I was slowly drifting into a deep, deadly pit. Then it all went black.

"So you had a dream about some tall shadow dude?" my best friend, Alex Jayman asked.

Fortunately for me, I happen to have a very realistic imagination during sleep. "I don't know. It just seemed . . . so . . . so real," I answered, shuddering just thinking about the strange incident. *What if the shadow figure is real? What if he's after me? Will anyone else see him? Am I going insane?* My thoughts swirled around my head like objects in a tornado. "Only you. Only you. Only you." Oh, no. It was happening again. "Only you. Only yoooou!"

Suddenly the sound stopped. The silence broke when someone started yelling my name. "Robert! Robert!" I snapped back into reality.

"Dude. What the heck?! You totally just spaced out," Alex said.

I grasped my forehead. It felt hot.

"Are you all right?" he asked.

"I feel like I'm gonna throw up," I answered.

"Come on. Let's take you to the nurse." He grabbed my hand and walked me to the health room.

"What's up, sweetie? You got a fever?" Ms. Anne, the nurse, asked.

"Yeah," I answered groggily. She stuck a thermometer in my mouth. She unfortunately said, "Oh yeah. 104. What's your mom's number?"

I coughed painfully and answered, "555-787-4639."

She tapped the numbers on the phone. The repetition of the clicking started to get on my nerves. Bad. Finally, the nurse stopped and started saying something to my mom. But whatever it was, I couldn't understand it. The darkness was starting to come back. "Only you. Only yo—Aughhh!"

I jolted into the air, sweating like I was wearing a jacket in 80-degree weather. My mom looked at me.

"Hey, sweetie. How are you feeling?" she asked.

"Wait, whuh?" I answered with a psychotic look on my face.

She chuckled. "Yeah. You were passed out when I got

there."

I stared at her. "Huh?"

She chuckled again. "Go to sleep, sweetie, it's late."

I gasped. "No! No, no, no, no. No. No."

She glared at me. This time it was her turn to look psychotic. "Okay, okay! Relax. Watch some TV or something." She started up the stairs and then stopped. "Tell me if you need anything, okay?"

"Kay." I answered. She started up again. "Wait!" I said.

"Yes?" she asked.

"Why did you tell me to sleep, after I'd been sleeping?" She shrugged with her pupils at the edge of her eyes and started up again.

The angry-looking cafeteria lady poured the green goop on my tray as I talked to Alex about what my mom had said.

"Yeah dude. Pretty peculiar indeed," he said with his eyebrow an inch above the other. We walked over to the 7th grade table. "You know, I always wondered about ol' Ms. Morganson."

I laughed.

"Your mom isn't exactly the most normal person out there." We dropped our trays on the table and sat down on the bench. I picked at my macaroni. "What's the matter, dude?" Alex asked. "You always love macaroni day."

I looked at Alex. "I don't know."

"All right, everyone. Open your history books to page 437 please," Mrs. Bowmanson said to our class.

I pulled my textbook out and flipped the pages over to 437. On the top of the page, in bright red letters, it said THE MAYFLOWER. I rolled my eyes. History was my least favorite class. Mrs. Bowmanson always droned on and on about how World War I started or what year the Declaration of

Independence was made. I know she's a teacher and all, but honestly, why not study about Basketball or try to find out learn who the voice of the Cookie Monster is or something?

"You said that to her face?" Alex asked me. We were at my house studying together. I had a guilty look on my face. Alex closed his book, and as soon as he saw my expression, he burst out laughing. "I can't believe you said that!"

I slapped my face. I knew I shouldn't have. "I'm guessing that had something to do with the *C-* I'd gotten on the big test yesterday."

Alex looked at the clock. "Oh, no. I should be getting home now. Later, dude!" Alex said, grabbing his backpack.

"Bye!" I yelled, as he left through the door.

I jumped in bed, pulled the covers over me, and fell asleep. A long silence. "Only you. Only you." I saw the figure again. I wasn't at my house anymore. I was in the dark forest again. This was it. I was over it. "Stop it!" I yelled. I stood up and walked over to the figure. I formed my hand into a fist. "Tell me what this is," I said. "Or else." He lifted his arm. His hand facing horizontal. Without any physical contact, a force hit me and I flew into the air and fell on my back against the dirt, not paralyzed, but barely able to move. He walked up to me. I was finally able to make out his face. A very familiar one. "Only you," he said with toothless sinister smile. I screamed.

2007

"There's no way that story's true," my new friend, Andrew Wayside said. "Oh, but it is." I said. "Only you." He glared at me. "What?" "Only you," I repeated. He laughed. I could tell he saw the red glowing in my eyes. A frightened look grew on his face. This was just what I wanted. "You don't understand. I'm Robert Morganson." His eyes widened. "But I thought the shadow person was the bad guy," he said, getting more and more scared. "*Was*, Andrew. He was. Until of course, he got me." He started backing away from me. "Hey, Alex, it's time." Alex walked over from the side of the doorway to the empty cafeteria. "Welcome to the group, Andrew." Andrew backed away more. He hit the side of the wall. Alex and I cornered him. I held up my hand. The force that impacted me ten years ago was now impacting him. "What's happening?" he asked, rubbing his eyes groggily. He was panting heavily. He looked up. His panting silenced. Red formed in his eyes. He started to grin. Not just any grin. A toothless, sinister grin.

Portal

By Allie Nichols

Douglas Gardens Elementary School

Purr. Purr.

I wake up to see my cat Chloe on my chest, purring as loud as a hair dryer. As I yawn and look at my clock beside my bed, I see—it's 8:00! School starts at 8:05! I rush up, pushing Chloe, causing her to run off, and get a decent outfit to change into for a day. I run out the door of my room to make my lunch and fill my water bottle. I open the door and see Chloe in a box next to the door.

"Bye, Mum!" I yell and assume she hears me. I put my backpack on and run out the door.

I run down the sidewalk and don't see any crossing guards for the school. I look both ways to see not a single car passing. I run out in the road, drop my backpack—and freeze. I look all around and everything is frozen. I see a darkish-purple hole that looks like a galaxy, maybe a few feet higher than me. "A portal?" I think to myself. Suddenly everything unfreezes and I trip, falling into the portal and I vanish.

I wake up in an unknown area resting on the cold grass. I lift myself up to see a big jungle-wood sign that's a few feet high that says, "WELCOME." I look around me to see nothing but tall grass and some big thick logs. I look behind me and see a whole ocean with a small island about a mile away. *Plop!* I look more into the water to see a calico cat in the water struggling to swim but can't. I rush to the water, grabbing the cat while seagrass is moving through my feet and the bottom on my legs. I huddle the cat closer to my chest to get the warmth back. I get back on land and sit down, with the cat in my lap purring with contentment. I grab the logs and some dry grass, tying the logs to make some sort of raft. After that, I slowly fall asleep with the cat by my side.

"I'll name you Anna," I say to myself as I fall asleep.

I wake up with Anna on my chest and the sun just starting to rise. I pick her up to put her beside me. I get up to see a beautiful sunrise and . . . horses in the distance? I take a few steps forward to see more of the view. I crunch on some dead grass and a horse looks over.

"There's about five horses," I whisper to myself while I walk closer with excitement. The horses seem friendly.

A horse prances over. He has a black mane and a caramel brown body with white spots all over. As he stops in front of me, confused as if I was made up, he snorts. As he kinda shoves me with his long nose, I pet him on the head. He snorts again. As the sun rises more, he fades.

"Can I only see him at night?" I think to myself.

He fades even more, until the sun is all the way up and he fades away in pieces. I look back to see Anna still asleep. Walking over, I watch her slowly awaken. I sit next to her, getting some grass to tie on the bottom of the "raft" I made last night. I look out in the distance in the water and see a small red crab crawling out of the water chasing another crab that's more orange than red. I grab the orange one and put it in the water again. The red one again vanishes into the water.

I look out into the sea and see the little island in the distance. I get up, grab the little raft, put it into the water, and sit on it. It holds me. I get off, grabbing the raft and pulling it out of the water. I pick up Anna and say, "We're going to that island. Over there!" I say pointing out into the distance. "I have a raft and everything! And on the island, I see great big trees—those must be coconut trees!"

I grab some more grass and left over sticks. I put the raft in the water and sit down on it. It barely holds me. A little bit of water spills in and Anna sprints higher, getting on top of my shoulders. I paddle with my hands making little waves in the water. I cup my hands as if they were paddles so the raft will move faster. I stop for a moment and have the waves pull me farther out to sea. I lie down and Anna walks down the raft leaving little water puddles that the grass slurps up in a second. I lie on my stomach to see the water as clear as fresh glass with all different colors of coral surrounding the bottom of the ocean floor. I watch fish swim by with little fish following behind them. Closer to the bottom, I see a stingray pass with a long tail following behind as it swoops under me. I slowly fall asleep with Anna on my back, also falling asleep.

~ *cRaCK!* ~ The raft hits something, tearing it apart, and water starts flowing in. Anna falls in meowing. It's the island! Grabbing her wet fur and putting her on the island, I grab onto a log, pulling myself to shore, and smacking my hands against fresh shells pulled in from the waves. I get on land and see a whole coconut in front of my face. I rush up, grabbing the coconut and walking to a huge rock nearby, and struggle to crack open the coconut. I finally open it, chug it, and looking down, I see a three-foot sea turtle looking up at me. I stumble down with confusion on my face. Looking up, I see a coconut falling from a nearby tree and it hits my head.

I wake up hearing a loud fan next to me, and smell fresh pancakes and tea. I open my eyes and look around.

"My room?" I think to myself. "How am I in my room?

Was I just dreaming?"

I jump out of bed and swing my door open. I run to the kitchen almost tripping myself and I see . . . my mum! She's here! I rush over to hug her as tightly as possible. I let go and grab a pancake and munch on it.

"Good morning, Allie!" Mum says.

I keep silent. She won't believe my dream. I'm sure it's real.

"When you were asleep, a calico cat stopped by and I fed her. She's inside right now exploring!" Mum says. "Want to name her—"

"ANNA! I wanna name her Anna."

"Anna it is," Mum replies.

Clones

By Elizabeth Meigs

Marist High School

There was nothing; a void. She floated in emptiness, feeling nothing, seeing nothing, just being. She sat in her tank, her own personal slice of the world, eyes closed. The fluid around her body lifted her, making her float. The number on her tank read "A24W7Z." The closest she'd ever come to an identity.

There was nothing. Then all of a sudden, there was something. She sat up with the force of it, memories, dreams, feelings all flooding her brain. She felt their names as she experienced each one in return, but remained unsure of what they were. She thrashed her body around, trying to escape the hold on her mind, but this thing had dug its claws in deep. A mother kissing her child, an old man blowing out candles on a cake, a puppy, now aged in the next snapshot as the kids grew with him. She shook her body, willing herself to escape, only managing to spill water everywhere in her violent fit.

Next, she was a kid in a classroom, cheating on a quiz. Her chest tightened at the feeling of it, emotions overcoming her. But now, look! She was outside, a small girl bundled up, enjoying her day off from school and playing in the snow. She reached her hand out, mesmerized by the white flakes falling from the sky. One came close, and kissed her palm as it fizzled out into nothingness. The vision pinned her in place and she lay, limbs stilled, unable to move, only able to take in a ragged breath, exhaling it in the next moment.

She was now an older girl on the cusp of adulthood, sitting in a church, heavy with the anguish of loss. She now felt herself unable to breathe, and her heart hurt in ways she'd never experienced, and she clawed at her chest to make it stop.

Suddenly, as soon as it had come, everything vanished, and she was pulled back to reality and her small tank.

A gasp of air, then a second.

The strange experience relaxed its hold, and she was finally able to move. The whole thing left her feeling emptier than before. But it still left her feeling something.

What did this all mean? Why her? Why now?

She sat up in her small pool with the sudden urge to get out. She needed out. It felt like the chamber walls around her were closing in, suffocating her. A24W7Z didn't know what to do, but she took the moment to still her breathing and examine her surroundings.

Looking around, she remembered that she was not the only one there. In fact, many shallow pools fanned out before her, behind her, and all other directions. She could see the familiar figures floating absently in each pool. Each figure exactly the same, lying face up, all body parts covered in a shallow casing of water that stopped below their noses. She reached up and touched her own features in recognition of the bond they all shared.

She remembered the faces, the face. It was cold and callous, set with wide doe eyes, and a deceptively innocent looking pair of lips. The face, sewn onto each body, each being, ended the thought of individuality and enforced sameness. She thought about that cruel face.

Her face.

A thought crossed her mind, and it happened so quickly, she was startled and fell out of the tank. "This is wrong," she thought. She wasn't sure how her mind, meant for rational thinking, and hardwired with facts, came to the conclusion, but there it was. A sickly sensation overcame her, and she realized the evil around her. She thought back to the vision of the kid cheating on a test. The feeling was similar, only one hundred times worse.

But still, the fact that she was even having thoughts and ideas was absurd.

As she lay on the cold ground outside of her safe pool, she felt herself shrink, pulling her knees close to her chest and wrapping her arms around her slim body. Little tremors fired off like a canon all over her, and she shook, burying her head under her arms. She remembered one of her visions, the one with the kid and the snow. The feeling was similar, and she realized with a start that she was cold.

"I need to fix this," she said, her voice hoarse from little use.

Suddenly, she heard a loud scratching noise, as if heavy metal was being dragged along a surface. Then, a light padding noise. 1, 2, 1, 2, 1, 2. A pair of footsteps.

She looked down at herself, and was—what was the word? Oh, yes, embarrassed. She was embarrassed looking at her naked body, with nothing to clothe herself in the near vicinity. This normally wouldn't have mattered, but now?

The footsteps grew in volume, increasing just as she tried desperately to make herself smaller.

The footsteps stopped. There was a warm hand on her bare back, and she shivered as she leaned into that touch.

"A24W7Z, are you well?" The girl sitting on the floor thought a moment. What did "well" mean?

"I—" She tried again, willing her voice to still. "I feel different." She looked up at the girl standing beside her, seeing the face twisted into a confused expression.

"I wonder if you caught the virus going around. We have a weakened immune system, you know." Yes, that must be it! She wasn't going crazy after all! A virus was to blame for these strange dreams, these visions she couldn't shake. She nodded in agreement.

"Here, I'll help you up and escort you to the medical wing." A24W7Z stood on shaking legs, wrapping her arms around her chest, making a shield against the frigid air.

"So cold," she muttered to herself as she walked beside her escort. The other girl paused, frozen like the air of the room.

"What did you just say?" the other girl said slowly, a threat of danger lacing her words.

"Nothing, I just was wondering how long to the medical wing." The girl looked back at her. An unusual expression crossed her face, but it was gone moments later, and her face, their face, returned to a neutral, pleasant facade. A24W7Z wasn't sure why she felt the need to cover up her misstep, but she saw something in that girl's face, felt a prick of fear that had her arm hairs standing up straight when she tensed.

The pair of girls made their way out the metal doors that led to the rest of the compound, and started down a pristine white hallway. Other girls passed them on their journey, all the same blank expression, every girl identical to the last. A24W7Z suddenly felt completely alone in the sea of bodies.

All too soon, the girls arrived at the medical wing, and they were ushered into a room. Thankfully, her escort requested a set of clothes for A24W7Z to wear and she put them on greedily, happy to have a barrier between her and the others.

A doctor came in moments later, and the doctor's face mirrored theirs. The doctor smiled slightly. "A24W7Z, is it?"

She nodded a yes. "Good, now what seems to be the problem?" The doctor took a seat in front of them, and the girl glanced between her and her escort, unsure of where to begin. Before she had too much time to think about it, the girl beside A24W7Z launched into the story for her.

"I was doing my routine checks of the sleeping pods, when I noticed that there was a disturbance with one. I found A24W7Z on the ground just outside her pod. It seemed to me that she may have the virus."

The doctor pursed her lips thoughtfully. "If that's the case, I should be able to run a test to confirm, and then give you instructions on how to heal up."

A24W7Z bobbed her head in agreement.

The doctor got up from her chair and opened a cabinet to grab a syringe. The girl felt a shudder through her. Usually needles didn't bother her, but today she didn't want it anywhere near her.

"Are you sure this is necessary? I think I'm feeling better already," A24W7Z exclaimed as she stood, eager to keep distance between the doctor and herself.

"Relax. There is obviously something wrong with you. I just have to make sure you have the virus before I give you anything." Before she could escape, the doctor grasped her arm and guided her body back into a sitting position. It took every ounce of willpower she had not to sprint away.

As the needle drew nearer to the junction between her arm, A24W7Z sat straight up and held her breath. She didn't like it one bit.

"Huh, you are acting very odd," the doctor said. Then she plunged the needle straight into her.

The girl tried not to think about the doctor and her close proximity. She stared straight at the wall and pretended to be interested in the diagram displayed there. But all she could think about were the visions she was trying so hard to ignore.

They weren't normal, and they simply didn't make sense.

What felt like forever ended when the doctor released her hold on the girl's arm and withdrew the needle. A24W7Z gasped, releasing the breath she was holding in. The doctor only gave her another strange look.

"I'm going to test your blood for the virus. I'll be back shortly." The doctor exited the room. The two girls sat there patiently waiting for the results. Small talk was usually discouraged, so the escort pulled out her tablet, presumably to get some work done, while the other girl just stared at the diagrams opposite her, which featured the muscular, skeletal, and nervous systems.

A24W7Z was halfway through memorizing the muscles poster when the doctor re-entered the room. The doctor looked down at her clipboard and sighed.

"As far as I can tell, nothing is wrong with you. You don't have the virus, and all your vitals are normal. I don't know what to tell you." A24W7Z frowned. Was there really nothing wrong with her? Then why did she still feel so weird?

She debated with herself on whether or not she should reveal the real reason she was out of her pod. What would the doctor say? Would she believe her? She finally decided that she had to tell somebody, even if they didn't believe her.

"I . . . " she began, unsure of where she was going with this. "I saw something earlier, while I was in my pod." She felt the doctor's and girl's heads snap to her, and she knew she had their undivided attention. "I don't know what to call it. But I saw things that I've never seen. There was this dessert and these little sticks of fire stuck in it. I think it was called a birthday." The doctor and the girl said nothing, only widened their eyes. A24W7Z took this as a hint to continue.

"And there was this white stuff falling from the sky, I think the word was snow. It was unlike anything I ever felt before." She paused. "I felt cold." At this, the doctor stepped forward, and the girl stood. They glanced between her and each other, murmuring. They looked like two scheming twins standing there together. A24W7Z caught snippets of their conversation, but only the words "awake" and "impossible."

Their increasingly inquisitive faces only served to worsen the panic she began feeling when she walked through the medic doors an hour ago. Slowly, A24W7Z lifted herself out of the plastic chair. The pair stopped conversing immediately, giving her their full attention.

"I think I should go, maybe get some more rest."

"No, I think it would be best if you stayed. I know just the thing you need," the doctor said, eyeing her up and down like she was a curious science experiment. Her steel gaze was unnerving.

The girl started towards the door anyway, not liking the tone of the doctor's voice and her storm cloud eyes. A24W7Z tried to push towards the door, but the pair grabbed her and walked her to the table.

"No! Please let me go! I'm fine!"

"No, you're not. You're very sick. Please remain calm." The doctor's words did nothing to console the thrashing girl. They pushed her on the table, and before she had the chance to escape, the girl who escorted her pulled out restraints hidden underneath the examination table.

A24W7Z saw these and bucked like a wild horse. There was no way she was going to willingly let someone put those awful things on her. But, unfortunately for her, two are stronger than one, and they eventually pinned her arms enough to tie them down. The legs were next to go, and the harsh leather dug into the soft skin of her ankles. The last was a thick band that was secured tightly around her waist to keep her in place.

She felt the tears rolling down her face. She had never felt this immense feeling of fear before. The unknown scared her. She heard the doctor roaming around the room looking for tools and closed her eyes as another tear managed to escape. She thought back to her visions to distract her. The snow, the test, the cake. She wouldn't take any of it back. It was the only thing different, the only interesting thing ever to happen in her gray life. Every day was the same blur with the same face. The same person replicated as different beings. The same manipulation.

It seemed the doctor had found what she was looking for, and the girl strapped to the table glimpsed a shiny glass bottle and another needle. The doctor inserted the needle into the fluid and filled it completely. She walked toward the exam table and stopped when she saw the tears staining the girl's face.

"Please, there's nothing wrong with me. Don't take them away."

The doctor sighed. "This is not what you were meant to be, and you are of no service with your own thoughts and feelings."

Before the girl could protest again, the doctor rammed the needle into her skin, and she felt herself slipping, fading. She let out a breath and relaxed onto the parchment paper beneath her. It didn't feel painful, and she wasn't scared anymore. In fact, it didn't feel like anything.

She relaxed her head first, then let her shoulders drop, the nothingness flooding south. She unclenched her fists, released tension in her stomach, and felt her legs become heavy.

She stared up at the cruel face above her, the same features plastered onto her own face. She hated that face.

But even that burning hatred faded, and she lay there, returned to the shell she was the previous day, unfeeling, unmoving.

"You are only worth something as a clone, not as an individual. Remember that."

Fan the Flames

When the Sun Goes Down

By Natasha Dracobly

South Eugene High School

"They say we're gonna die."

Callie's hair looks like neon flames in the sunlight, even brighter than last time I saw her. She kicks her feet against the station wall, first her left foot, then her right. Thump. Thump. Callie always kicks things when she's thinking.

"Sure do," she says finally, after kicking the wall a few more times. She doesn't look over at me.

"Well?"

Thump. Thump. "Well what?"

"Well, what do you think?" I know I sound nervous. I look away from her, twirling a strand of my hair around my finger. The wind on our faces feels colder today than usual. I push my hair out of my face, but the wind just blows it back again. It makes me angry for some reason. I kick the wall, too.

The station here is really more like a shack. It's been Callie's and my hideout since we were kids. Here, we'd laugh and run around without worrying about the gods watching us, or the rules we had to follow in the City. Here, we could just be ourselves. We'd climb up on the roof just like today, point at the setting sun and pretend we were great explorers. Callie would walk along the very edge of the roof, her feet only half-touching the tiles. I'd pull her away.

It's been a while since I've been up here. It's been a while since I've seen Callie, too. When I sent the message today, we hadn't talked in months. Now, looking at her, she's the complete opposite of everything I've become. She always refused to conform to what the City said. She never listened to the prophets. I suppose I shouldn't have been too surprised when she ran away completely.

"I thought they didn't want you to think." Callie still doesn't look at me. I can't even see her face now; the wind keeps blowing her hair in front of it. I think I might be angry at her.

I kick the wall again, harder this time. "Ow!"

She laughs, and turns a bit further towards me. I almost think she's going to look at me, but she doesn't. Her gaze stops at my shoes. She flicks her hand towards them. "You're wearing City shoes. You can't kick walls with boots like that."

"Who says I can't?" I kick the wall again. It hurts. I glare at my feet.

"Common sense," she says. Callie loves to talk about common sense.

"Whatever." I'm still angry. At Callie, at the City, at the prophets, at the gods. I can hardly tell at this point. I glance at the sun.

Maybe I'm paranoid, but it looks lower on the horizon than before.

I try to talk slower this time. Callie probably thinks I sound hesitant. Callie always used to say I sounded that way. It felt like she'd interrupt me once a minute at least to tell me to sound more confident. She never had any issues with sounding confident, of course. She was the leader. I was always happy to follow.

"If you only had a few hours left to live . . ." Callie's not an idiot. She knows what I'm saying here. I twist my hair tighter around my fingers. "If you only had a few hours left to live, what would you do?"

She kicks the wall again with her nice wall-kicking boots. Thump. Thump. I glance at the sun again.

"Talk about a heavy question."

I laugh. It sounds harsh, harsher than I ever sound. Maybe Callie's rubbing off on me. "Well, you don't have forever to answer it."

She looks up at the sun, too, hot and blazing in the bright blue sky. The sky never looks this blue in the City. I should come out here more often.

That is, if I'm still alive.

Callie stares into the distance. She was always good at blankly staring at things while she thought. She used to stare at me. Now she refuses even to look my way. "I guess, if I was gonna die, I'd stop worrying about my job, or money, or the City rules. I'd just do what I wanted." She shrugs. "But those are the things we live by out here anyway. If you really wanna let go of the City, you don't have to die to do it."

I almost say something, but the way she's sitting, with her shoulders a bit hunched up, staring into the sky like she's afraid, makes me stay quiet. Callie is never afraid.

"If you're gonna die, and you know it, you should let go of whatever kind of expectations you've got on you. I mean, none of it'll matter when you're dead." She pauses again. "I'll tell you that. I'd never be able to do that myself."

If we were like before, I'd go and sit down right next to her, and put my arm around her shoulder, and we'd just sit like that. We might talk, but mostly we'd just be there. Close together. Holding on.

But we aren't like before. We aren't anything, really, so I just look in her direction as I talk. "Callie, you're better at dropping expectations than anyone. I mean, look at you. Look at how you've let go of the City."

Callie shakes her head. Her hair flies around her face. She's still looking at the sky. I just wish she'd look at me. I think everything might be all right then. "That's different. You've got the expectations of the City on you. The expectations on me these days are different."

"What are they?"

"You wouldn't understand."

I nod. "Okay." I probably wouldn't. Callie's probably right.

She stands up. She looks like a statue like this, silhouetted before the sun. I'd follow her anywhere.

"Are you leaving?" This conversation has been awkward, but I don't think it's been that awkward. I hope she doesn't leave. I don't really want to count down the minutes to my death alone.

"No." She doesn't elaborate. "The sun's getting pretty low."

I nod. "Yeah."

"Not so many hours now. More like minutes. Not so much time to do things."

"Yeah."

I stand up, too. I'm a little closer to her now.

"So, what exactly did the prophets say? Just out of curiosity."

"Right." Callie's always been one for gallows humor. "To pass the time."

She grins. It fades quickly. "Exactly."

I shrug my shoulders and stare resolutely at the sky. "They didn't say much, to be honest. Just that when the sun goes down tonight, everyone who doesn't believe in the gods will die."

"Well, you don't need to worry then, do you? You believe."

"I'm afraid of the gods. It's not the same as believing."

"It's basically the same."

I shrug again. "Maybe."

The sun is really very low now. Its light barely stretches to meet the dust that covers everything we can see. The stars are coming out now. I can see the moon.

"How long do you think we have? A couple minutes? Less?"

"Less."

I count in my head. One second, two seconds, three seconds. I watch the light fade until it's gone. My heart is beating faster than it ever has.

"Nothing!" I turn to Callie. "We're fine, you were right!"

I reach to hug her just as she falls. She's dead before she touches the tiles.

I don't know what I do. I don't know what I scream. I'm sure I scream. I don't know anything. I know that somehow I got her off the roof, got both of us off the roof. I know I've been digging in the dirt by the station so long my hands are bleeding, and nothing has happened to me still. I'm still alive. My hands are bleeding, but I'm still alive.

I stand up. I'm coming back to Callie. I'm going to bury her. But first, I have to get a shovel, and maybe some bright red hair dye.

The No Named Soldier

By Peyton Tyner

Eugene Christian School

"RPG!" someone yelled. . . . *BOOM!!!*

A massive explosion capsized the rear member of the convoy, followed by several more missiles that caused the other two trucks to erupt into flames. Only my vehicle was left unharmed, but I knew that it would not be long before another incoming missile blew it up. I grabbed my partner, John Stephens, by the arm and pulled him over to me, before nearly tackling him off the back side of the armored truck less than a second before it was hit by a missile. The blast from the explosion sent me flying backward nearly forty feet, and the shock of the event made me lose grip on John.

I hit the ground incredibly hard, sending a sharp pain throughout my body. Then everything went black as I tumbled across the sand, and I was out cold, lying like a fish out of water.

* * *

While I was out, I remembered a very specific point in my life that changed the way I thought about the world. I was nine years old. My dad told me he was going to be back before I knew it; he even promised it. But when I heard a knock and answered the door to a pair of soldiers, I received the horrible news. My mom was not far behind me when the soldiers took their eyes off me and looked at my mom. They did nothing but shake their heads when my mom cupped her face with her hands and began to cry. Then I realized what had happened: He was gone. I would never see his face, listen to his jokes, or hear his voice again. He was gone for good, and all that I could do, being a Christian boy, was blame God for his death. I never stopped to think that he was in a better place now. A place without evil or anger. A place without fighting or war. A place of peace and serenity. Until one day, I thought about this and decided I was going to do something to make this world a better place.

Ten years later, I joined the military, and two years after that, I was assigned this mission. What I believe is that if you don't know the names of whoever died, there would be no sorrow or mourning, which is why I became the No Named Soldier in remembrance of my father, and I would stick with that title until my last breath.

* * *

The memory faded as my consciousness returned to me and I began to see the real world again. I shifted my head and saw half of my body layered in sand and the other half hidden by a long metal scrap of one of the trucks. As I struggled to free myself from the earth's grasp, I remembered my partner. I began to vigorously dig my way to the top of the sand and almost shed tears as I struggled to bring myself to my feet. But it was no use. I was unable to escape the natural trap and live on my father's legacy, so I allowed myself to calm down and stop trying . . . until I heard a cry for help.

"Please!" a faint voice cried in the distance. "Somebody help me!"

"John!" I called back. A sense of urgency filled my body, and after less than five seconds of struggle, the metal scrap began to budge. Inch after inch, I was able to push the chunk of the vehicle into the earth beside me. I scraped the remnants of dust off my body and lifted myself to my feet before nearly collapsing back into the sand from the loss of blood. I glanced down at my leg to see a long scar-to-be that stretched across the top of my thigh.

Grimacing at the pain, I limped over to where I heard the call from, and saw John lying in the sand with a look of horror on his face. I examined his body from yards away and saw multiple metal shards and rods piercing his abdomen. Cuts and bruises marked his face beyond recognition, but when he turned his head and saw me standing only yards from him, excitement replaced the pain, and the thought of rescue overthrew him.

"John!" I cried again, dashing as fast as I could to his resting place.

"I thought that I lost you, soldier," I told him.

"Well, I'm glad that you didn't," he joked.

I knelt beside him and surveyed the land for something of use. A first-aid kit would have been a miracle. I told John that I was going to go look for supplies and that I would not take long, but it took nearly ten minutes only to find some gauze, a half-empty flask, and a Glock 17 holding thirteen rounds.

I wrapped the gauze around my wounded leg and returned to John.

"Not so long, huh?" he asked.

"Sorry, I couldn't find much, but at least I can wrap your wounds with this gauze," I took the water bottle from my utility belt and handed it to John. "Here, drink this."

John took a sip of the bottle and cringed at the taste. "This isn't water," he said. "This is whiskey." He handed the bottle back to me.

"It will dull the pain." I poured the whiskey onto one of

the metal rods that pierced his abdomen and listened to his awful scream. Then I applied pressure to his chest and yanked the rod out in one quick motion trying not to cry from the sound of his screaming. I covered his piercings with gauze and lifted him to his one good leg to help him hobble back to the site of the crash.

* * *

"Who were those guys?" John asked as we scavenged for any supplies that I may have missed.

"S.C.O.R.P.I.A agents," I answered. "They must've known that we were coming. But how could they have known?"

"I don't know, but we need to find some cover for the night," John said looking up at the sky.

The sky was beginning its cycle from day to night as the red dusk sky slowly faded from sight and the black night became dotted with faint, white stars. I continued hitting my communications system with my fist, trying to receive a signal to call for backup. To our dismay, my radio was broken and the communications systems inside the vehicles were either destroyed or surrounded by flames.

"My comm system is busted," I said. "We got no way to contact headquarters."

"What do we do about the mission?" John asked.

"Going to Afghanistan? Please, we'll be lucky to find a place to sleep," I responded.

"There should be a town not far from here," John reassured me. "We can camp out there until morning."

"That should be fine as long as we don't run into any S.C.O.R.P.I.A agents."

"Or a bear," John joked, making me laugh for the first time all day.

* * *

Nightfall was at its peak when we finally reached the town, or what was left of it for that matter.

"What happened here?" John asked, concerned.

"Yeah, less of a town and more of a graveyard," I replied. "Come on, we should be able to find a building that's not in ruins."

We entered the town and wandered around until we found a half run-down house that was missing an entire story. The ground level floor acted as a fine place to stay for the night. I dragged John into the doorway and closed the remains of the door behind me when I heard the faintest sound in the distance. It sounded like a voice, but I was unable to make out any words. I ignored the disturbance after a short while of standing and scanning the horizon and sat down beside John.

"Let's just get some rest," John whispered.

"Yeah, you're right. I'll look for a way to contact headquarters in the morning and find some food and water." I rolled over in an attempt to fall asleep, but the sound of a stone rolling towards me interrupted it. I opened my eyes and glanced at the doorway. A shadow crossed through the crack of the door and stopped only seconds later. My heart began to race.

Someone's here, I thought.

I backed into the shadows as quietly as I could, when I heard John groan and reposition himself. I thought that whoever had been outside may have heard John.

"John," I whispered. "John."

No response came. I unholstered my pistol and positioned it in my hand while pointing it at the door, waiting for someone to set foot in the building.

Silence.

I began to lower my gun when I heard another set of footsteps.

They're not looking for us. I thought. *They're patrolling.*

I devised a plan to figure out who was here with us. I waited for the set of footsteps to pass directly in front of the door and then counted to 317 before I heard them again.

"Five minutes," I whispered to myself.

I counted again, but this time only to 265 before I heard the footsteps again.

"Four and a half." I thought for a moment before figuring out a logical conclusion. If I wait for two minutes after the footsteps return to my location, I could easily exit the building without any distress.

It's only about a third of a mile for them to walk, which gives me a clear opening at 142 seconds. . . . Agh, what am I doing? I glanced at my wrist before remembering that my watch had fallen off during the ambush.

Thinking about the ambush made me wonder how the S.C.O.R.P.I.A agents even knew the route we had taken. I brushed the thought aside and refocused on my current, self-devised mission.

I took position by the door and patiently listened for the passing patrollers. I held back for two minutes and then made my move.

I quickly dashed towards the nearest cover, which happened to be a burning truck similar to the one that I had been in. Realizing that I was easily visible, I stood for a few seconds behind the car, surveyed the area, and then sprinted to a tall, run-down building.

I ducked behind a trio of rusty barrels and peeked over the top when I spotted the returning soldiers. This time, instead of bypassing John's whereabouts, they paused under the nose of where John lay. I watched as they began to converse and occasionally glance back at the building.

I knew that I had to act fast if I wanted to keep John's position secure, so I decided to create a distraction. Searching the earth frantically for a useful object, I began to panic. I heard the soldiers talking louder and soon they began arguing amongst themselves, which handed me the time I needed to find a weathered can on the ground only feet from me. I peered back at the soldiers, who were only seconds from entering the building when I hurled the can near the soldiers to draw their attention away from the building and John.

I waited anxiously for a reaction from the soldiers. And then it came. The near second that I waited felt like an eternity as I watched the soldiers advance to where I had tossed the can. Then I continued on my way, heaving a sigh of relief.

* * *

After maneuvering through old, dilapidated buildings, I finally found the site where the central activity went down. Soldiers in uniform and heavily armed with illegal weapons loaded and unloaded trucks full of crates. I was unable to decrypt the writing on the crates, but I knew they contained items capable of unimaginable destruction.

The soldiers were S.C.O.R.P.I.A agents who had been transported from their main headquarters in Saudi Arabia to intercept my team's convoy before we reached our rendezvous point in Afghanistan.

The same question filled my mind for a moment. How could they have known where we were going to be and when we were going to be there? The thought left as soon as I heard another set of footsteps signaling that I was in imminent danger.

I emerged from my dark lookout point swiftly but silently as the footsteps approached.

I watched through a large crack in the wall to see only one soldier pass by.

I knew that I needed to get closer to the main site, so I rushed out of my enclosed hiding spot to attack the soldier. The soldier must have heard me approaching as he unholstered his pistol from his belt and turned around like a whirlwind and aimed his gun directly at my forehead.

Little did he know that I was a soldier and expected him to turn around, so I disarmed him before he could pull the trigger by grabbing his wrist and bending it to the point where his fingers gave out and dropped the gun. Then I took his clothes and utilities before I secretly infiltrated the compound. I wrapped a thin scarf around my face to conceal my identity and made my way over to the loading site.

I shook uncontrollably as I marched over to the loading site when a scrawny man wearing my exact outfit began to shout and yell foreign words in my direction. He approached me angrily, continuing to yell, when he finally pointed towards the unloading site and motioned me to go over there.

I nodded and hustled while trying to blend in. I grabbed a crate from the back of a truck and followed the other soldiers. We walked down a staircase into a dimly lit room. Shelves were stacked with weapons and handheld explosives lined the walls. I glanced to my left and saw a steel door with a square window dividing me and what seemed like an important room. I parted from the line of soldiers without anyone paying much attention. I took a deep breath before turning the doorknob and entering the room.

The room felt cold and brought a feeling of guilt upon me. The walls were empty and there was nothing but a wooden desk illuminated by a single lamp. My heart pounded as I approached it. On it sat a manila folder scarcely revealing a thin set of documents. I caught a glimpse of a nondescript figure on the corner of the page as I began to flip open the folder. I recognized the figure's bodily structure but I couldn't pin-point his name.

I continued reading until I skimmed over a paragraph that caught my eye. As I read, my thoughts wandered and my mind raced. I could not believe what I read.

It made sense, but I fought to accept it. It was impossible for me to accept. I just . . . couldn't. But then I came to my right mind and gave in to the truth.

John Stephens worked for S.C.O.R.P.I.A.

* * *

I played and replayed the past event in my head over and over as I raced back to John's location undetected.

John told them where we were going and how to stop us? The thought perplexed me. For what purpose? Money? Power?

Rage and disgust filled me as I thought up the most rational reasons for why my partner and best friend would betray me and the organization.

When I reached the rundown building, I forgot about the soldiers patrolling the site, but I could have cared less at that moment. I spotted the patrol officers out of the corner of my eye, and I reasoned that they saw me, too, because they pointed at me and began to run after me.

I panicked. Without thinking, I made a break for John's resting place only to find out that he was gone.

I cursed under my breath as I devised a plan to escape my pursuers. I hurried to a set of weathered stairs and bolted up them. Then I found a doorway to a separate room and waited out of sight of the staircase and stood by, until the soldiers entered the doorway.

As soon as I saw the barrel of his rifle enter the doorway, I pushed his gun to the side and kicked him down the stairs on top of his partner who was close behind. When I saw that they were thoroughly delayed, I continued to run back to the loading site.

When I reached the site to see John being escorted to a helicopter, I was furious and filled with adrenaline.

"JOHN!" I yelled as I sprinted towards the helicopter.

I evaded assault rifle shots and explosions as I dashed to my ex-partner, firing my thirteen rounds of pistol ammo at the origins of the bullets. I saw that few soldiers protected John, and that many of the bullets had stopped coming not long after.

I felt an instant sharp pain surge through my left shoulder, but I pressed on. I fired my final three rounds at John's escorts, which connected almost immediately, leaving John unharmed but on the ground clutching his abdomen.

I slowed down as I neared his resting place. Sweat dripped down my forehead as I removed my disguise from my face, and I breathed heavily as I approached John.

Panting, I said, "Why did you do it. Why did you betray me?"

No response.

"Why! John? For the money? The power? Why?"

"Go ahead, shoot me." John said from the ground grimacing. "I've brought you nothing but distress," he said. "I'll never be able to change what I messed up, so just . . . shoot me."

"I can't," I replied. "I won't."

"Just do it! Why can you not?!"

I lowered my gun. "Because I know your name."

A Dualistic Dichotomy

By Gracie Bratland

Churchill High School

Editor's note: This story includes domestic violence and suicide.

Her heart was beating in a harsh, choking staccato; he was there, in the stairwell. She detangled the bracelet from her shaky fingertips and dropped it into her apron pocket. Turning towards the cabinet she grabbed a bottle of vodka and a glass. The door swung open, "I need a drink."

"It's right here, just one moment."

He approached the counter, and propped himself up against it to watch her pour.

"Whatcha do today, my little matryoshka doll?"

"I was just cleaning at the plant, you know that I started working weekdays again. You drove me there for the interview, remember?" She finished pouring, and set the drink in front of him. He groped the glass and swirled it under his nose. "What the hell is this shit?"

"You haven't even tasted it yet. How can tell if it's bad or not?"

"Because it smells like cow piss."

"Well, I went down to the liquor store on Sixth Street like you told me."

"Damn it woman, I said Seventh! This—this is like the

trash that they hand out in the ration lines!" The veins on his forehead seemed to writhe under his skin, like bloodworms. Her mouth opened, but her throat was made of cement, so she looked down at her hands. They were like lace, tightly woven, bloodless.

"Well? What do you have to say for yourself? Hmm?" She focused her eyes on the warped wood floor.

"Fine then," he said, flinging the drink in her face. The cheap alcohol stung the corners of her eyes. It burned her sinuses. It tasted slightly of gasoline. He scanned her for a second, and then headed over to his recliner. With a certain pompous rhythm he plopped down, turned on the TV, and held the empty glass above his head for her to take.

The next day was gray. The apartment complexes, the street, the still water in the sink, they were all one entity: inevitable, impermeable, inexhaustible, imposturous, impending—The clock. It was 6:21 AM. She had some time. She could see him on the street below. The momentum of his briefcase pulled him deeper into the city, like a fat bass on a line. It made her smile, the belligerence in his bloated face was laughable.

She watched until he was completely drowned by the sea of heads. Gazing into the sink, she saw her mother's thin china plates, the glass from last night, some utensils, the fillet knife. It was 6:52. Time had escaped her, and now she was going to be late. It took fifteen minutes to get to the subway, there was a twenty-minute subway ride, and it took a few minutes from there to get to the plant. Work started at 7:30. She scampered around the apartment like a frightened mouse, snatching up her things, before rushing out the door.

By the time she had reached the metro, sweat had glued her thin black bangs to her forehead. Rather than repelling her perspiration, the frosted, dense fog inhibited the evaporation of any droplets from her skin. So she stood at the toll booth, panting, her sweat overwhelming her complexion in a mirage of translucent boils. The lady inside the booth was looking down at some papers and was tagged with a faded badge. The woman was slightly past middle age, had a gourd of a nose, and looked like she ate a lot of sausages; in fact, the woman resembled a sausage. After a few unnoticed seconds, she gave the glass between them three rapid knocks. The sausage looked up. "Do you need a ticket, or do you have a pass?"

"Uh, I have a pass, here—here, take it." Her voice was shaking as she thrust it through the slot. The woman rolled her eyes over the information on the card.

"OK, Ma'am. Looks like your train leaves in . . ." she checked her watch, "four minutes." The sedentary woman slid it back to her.

Taking the card, she muttered a breathless, "Thank you."

The fluorescent lights illuminated the train too well. Every stain on the faded paint, every vein of rust, every remnant of dirt, of food, of hair, she could see everything. Sitting with her ankles slanted to the left, she pulled the bracelet out from her purse, and placed it in the palm of her hand. It was a delicate little thing, gold plated, a little phosphorescent pearl strung onto it. Her father had given it to her when she was a little girl. It was very late when he came into her bedroom that night, still wearing his blue-gray officer uniform. "You awake, Sweetheart? I got you a gift." He then pulled it over her wrist and kissed her goodnight.

The train car came to a slow, screeching halt, a light flickered out, and the sliding door opened. Woken from her trance, she scrambled through the catacombs of the subway like a cockroach, frantically searching for the staircase that framed the power plant's three massive vases. She surfaced and ran. Her white breath and the white vapor that rose from the plant both bled into the sky. When she finally reached the entrance, she took a breath in and pulled on the door. A tepid, suffocating air rushed toward her. It was like a wet wool sock was crawling down her throat, burrowing into her lungs. She fell on the floor in chronic choking convulsions. She could feel the air ripping at the flesh of her esophagus, collapsing the walls of her trachea; fire with claws; a phoenix.

Her mind was clouded after that. She heard echoing murmurs. It smelled like floor cleaner. She felt two arms hooked under her shoulders, escorting her back outside. Out there, the air was crisp, and she tried to focus on the little diamonds of dew on the grass. A whisper fell on her ear, "We think that this job might be too demanding for you. We would appreciate it if you took your leave. No need to come back, we'll take care of your things," and with that, she floated back under the ceiling of stone, much like the ceiling of fog above it.

"Honey? Where ya at?" He turned his head toward the kitchen "Hun?" He peered down the dark hall and reached behind him to close the door. There was some disheveled black hair peeking out from his leather recliner. He set his briefcase down and walked over to her. "What are you doing?" Her eyes looked as if they had been veiled with the red-veined wings of a dragonfly. "Have you been crying? What do you even—"

"No."

"Don't lie. I don't need a hysteric who's a liar, too." He grabbed her arm. "Out with it."

"I was fired today."

He narrowed his eyes. "Of course you were." Then he slapped her across the face, hard. The veining on her eyes pulsed down to her cheek.

"Don't come into my room tonight," he said, and walked down the hallway.

There was a thud of the lock. She bolted up and traversed over to the kitchen with the tactful silence of a black cat. She began to sharpen the knife. Seven times on each side. She slid it across the meat of her thumb, a thin ruby line started to grow. Satisfied, she gathered the rest of the supplies and sat down at the kitchen counter. She started dialing.

It took fifteen minutes for the three leaden knocks to arrive at the door. Static. Three more knocks. Nothing. The door was kicked down, and an intense light escaped the room, blinding the officers. After rubbing the violent, shattered kaleidoscope from their eyes, they saw it. A litany of shouts ensued as they ran into the room, their wide eyes searching for the predator. The victim had a long knife pierced through the armor of their sternum, it must have been fractured in the process. It seemed as though they had dragged themselves towards the door after the fact; they had left a thick, sticky trail, like a snail. More barks, another door broken down, another struggle, another person silenced, captured, condemned. The procession then flooded out of the apartment, except for one officer, who remained in the doorframe. He turned back for one more look, and saw something white. He walked back over to the body and crouched down beside it. He maneuvered the bracelet over the stiff, twisted fingers.

It would be a great gift for his daughter.

Wayward Blazes

Stinkmutt and Trashcat

By Abbigail Park

River Road/El Camino del Río
Elementary School

Chapter One: The Rat in the Trashcan

One warm summer night, Stinkmutt and Trashcat—a husky and a white cat—were outside their farm in Vermont raiding the trashcan, when they met a rat who said he had traveled all over the U.S. Stinkmutt and Trashcat asked him where there was the most garbage, and he said it was New York City. Then they asked him what the fastest way to get there was.

"There is a garbage truck leaving in the morning. If you get in the trashcan at 7:00 am, you will be dumped into the garbage truck," said the rat. So at 6:56 the next morning, Stinkmutt and Trashcat got into the garbage can. A few minutes later, they were dumped into the garbage truck.

Stinkmutt and Trashcat liked it in the garbage truck. It was full of garbage to go through. They were also very excited. Stinkmutt could not stop imagining streets with heaps of garbage on them, and Trashcat could not help but think about streets lined with garbage cans overflowing with banana peels, old snack bags, and old soda cans. Then the truck came to a stop.

Chapter Two: New York City

Stinkmutt and Trashcat quickly got out of the truck and onto the street. There were not heaps of garbage like Stinkmutt had imagined. It was more like Trashcat was thinking, except there were not quite as many trashcans as he had been imagining. Trashcat was looking around at the tall buildings and Stinkmutt was looking for the biggest trashcan. Then Stinkmutt saw a person come out of a subway station.

"Hey, Trashcat," said Stinkmutt. "Let's go see what is down those stairs."

"Ok," said Trashcat. "Let's go!"

They went down the stairs into the subway station. When they got into the subway station, Stinkmutt saw some garbage on the tracks so he and Trashcat went to check it out. Then Stinkmutt heard the sound of a train. He looked down the tunnel and saw a subway speeding toward them.

"Trashcat, we need to get out of here!" said Stinkmutt.

"Why!?" said Trashcat.

"Because look down the tunnel, Trashcat!!!" Stinkmutt yelled.

"OH, NO!!!!!" screamed Trashcat, "WHAT ARE WE GOING TO DO?!?!"

"I have literally no idea!!!"

"We are going to get hit by the train!!!" yelled Trashcat.

"Wait!" said Stinkmutt, "I have an idea! There is a lever right there. If we pull it, then the train will be sent in a different direction!"

"It's worth a try," said Trashcat. Stinkmutt pulled the lever, and the train was sent in a different direction.

"We did it!!!" they shouted together. They quickly got off the tracks and climbed the stairs to the street.

"That was a close one," said Trashcat.

"Very close," agreed Stinkmutt.

Chapter Three: Tom the Dogcatcher

It was nighttime; the sky was dark, but the streets were lit from the lights of the buildings as Stinkmutt and Trashcat went through the garbage. Then all of a sudden, a man came running down the street.

"Who are you?" asked Stinkmutt.

"I am Tom, Tom the dogcatcher, and you are under arrest," he said importantly.

"Why?" asked Stinkmutt.

"Because you are on the street without an owner."

"So?" said Trashcat.

"It is not allowed in New York, and you are under arrest. Now come with me."

"Not likely!" said Stinkmutt. He and Trashcat ran.

"Get back here this instant!" shouted Tom.

"Do you really think we are going to stop?" yelled Stinkmutt.

"Well, no. But just stop!" said Tom. "Stop in the name of the law! I SAID STOP IN THE NAME OF THE LAW, AND THAT MEANS YOU NEED TO STOP!!!" But they were already gone, and several people were looking out their windows at Tom.

"WHAT?!" he yelled "I AM A DOGCATCHER AND I AM DOING MY JOB!!!"

"Dogs do not talk to people or understand them!" shouted one person.

"Yeah!" said someone else.

Chapter Four: Central Park

Stinkmutt and Trashcat ran and ran, turning onto new streets or alleys every few minutes. They eventually stopped running and looked all around to make sure Tom was not sneaking up on them. Then Trashcat looked down the street and saw what looked like a forest in the middle of the city.

"Hey, Stinkmutt, look at that forest."

"Oh, yeah."

"We could spend the night there. If Tom is still following us, he could not find us in there. It looks very big," said Trashcat.

"Good idea."

Stinkmutt and Trashcat ran down the street to the forest. When they got to the forest, they saw a sign that said CENTRAL PARK.

"That forest is called Central Park," said Stinkmutt.

"Cool," said Trashcat.

They followed a path that led them into Central Park. The park was very dark and a little creepy. Stinkmutt and Trashcat stayed very close together on the path. After a while they saw a big lake and went over to it. They were very thirsty from running so much. After drinking from the lake, they went back to the path and kept walking. Soon they saw a nice clearing in the woods that was surrounded by some big rocks.

"Let's spend the night here," said Trashcat.

"Okay," said Stinkmutt. They went to the center of the clearing and lay down, but they could not sleep; they had so much on their minds. All of a sudden, they saw a big shadow in the trees.

"Oh, no," said Trashcat.

"Who is there?!" said Stinkmutt. "Are you friends or foes?"

"It is ok," said a voice. "We are friends." A dog and a cat emerged from the trees.

"Oh!" said Trashcat. "I'm so sorry. You scared me for a minute."

"It is ok," said the dog. "My name is Olivia."

"It's nice to meet you Olivia. My name is Trashcat."

"And I'm Stinkmutt."

"Nice to meet you, Stinkmutt and Trashcat," said Olivia. The cat, who was fluffy and white, walked up to Stinkmutt and Trashcat.

"My name is Snowy," said the cat. "It is nice to meet you."

"So why are you hiding out in the forest?" asked Olivia.

"We are visiting from Vermont and are hiding from a dogcatcher named Tom." Stinkmutt explained.

"The dogcatcher's name is Tom?" Snowy asked.

"Yeah. Why? Do you know him?" asked Trashcat.

"Oh, we know Tom all right," said Olivia.

"How do you know him?" asked Stinkmutt.

"We were walking down the street, and he came up and tried to arrest us because we didn't have an owner, which is NOT a rule by the way," said Snowy.

"Ha ha! That's pretty much what he did to us," said Trashcat. Olivia and Snowy showed them how to make a fire by rubbing sticks or rocks together, and then they all went to sleep.

Chapter Five: The Statue of Liberty

Stinkmutt and Trashcat woke up the next day and walked around Central Park with Snowy and Olivia. It was a very warm and sunny day, so they decided to splash around in one of the lakes in the park. Then they snuck into a bagel shop before it opened and stole some bagels.

"These are the best bagels I've ever had!" exclaimed Stinkmutt.

"New York is known for its bagels," said Olivia.

"Oh! Olivia, we should show them the Statue of Liberty!" said Snowy.

"Oh, yeah. Good idea!" said Olivia.

"I would LOVE to see the Statue of Liberty!" said Trashcat.

"We would not just see it, you can go to the top of it," said Snowy.

"What's the Statue of Liberty?" asked Stinkmutt.

"Come ON, Stinkmutt. You have never heard of the Statue of Liberty? You MUST have," said Trashcat.

"Well I've HEARD of it. I just don't know what it is."

"We'll show you, come on!" said Snowy.

"How will we get there?" asked Trashcat.

"We'll show you that, too!" said Snowy.

"Wait!" said Olivia. "I need to get the rope!"

"Oh, yeah! Hurry up!" said Snowy. Olivia went to the side of the bagel shop and got a rope from behind one of the trashcans.

"Why do we need rope?" asked Stinkmutt.

"You will see," said Olivia.

They all started walking down the street. After a half an hour or so, they reached Battery Park where there were people boarding ferryboats.

"This way," Olivia whispered. She led the others through the crowd of people to one of the ferries.

"All right, Snowy, you know what to do," said Olivia. Snowy took the rope in her mouth, climbed up the side of the boat, and tied the rope to the handrail that was on top of the boat.

"Got it!" Snowy called.

"Okay, now follow me and do exactly what I do," said Olivia. She climbed up the rope to the top of the boat, and

Stinkmutt and Trashcat followed.

"That was cool," said Trashcat.

"It took us about ten tries to figure it out," said Snowy. Then the boat started to move.

"I'm so excited!" said Trashcat.

"Me, too!" Stinkmutt said.

"Look! There it is!" Olivia exclaimed.

"Oh, THAT'S the Statue of Liberty? Yeah, I've seen pictures of it. I mean who hasn't?!" said Stinkmutt.

Trashcat rolled his eyes.

After ten minutes or so, they got to Liberty Island.

"Now, let's climb down this rope," said Olivia.

Stinkmutt, Trashcat, and Olivia climbed down the rope, then Snowy untied the rope and jumped down.

"Wow, what a great view!" exclaimed Trashcat.

"It is even better from the top," said Snowy.

They walked around the island for a few more minutes and then found some trees to hang out by.

"So what is our plan?" asked Trashcat.

"We'll wait around here for a few hours. At six o'clock they close and lock the doors, so around five-fifty, we'll go inside and hang out in there until everyone leaves and then go up," said Olivia.

"All right," said Stinkmutt. "Sounds good."

It was already four-forty; they only had an hour and twenty minutes until six o'clock. They lay down and talked for a while. Then at five-fifty, they made their way over to the statue. They found the door and went inside the base of the statue. The inside was a small museum; there were models and pictures of how the statue was built.

"Over here," said Snowy. She led them over to one of the tables that was covered with a light blue cloth. Snowy crawled under the table and the others followed.

"What time is it?" asked Trashcat. Olivia poked her head out from under the table.

"Six o'clock," she responded. They heard a soft click as the door shut, and the turning of a key as the last person exited the building. They got out quickly and climbed up the stairs. When they reached the top of the base, they took another much narrower, steeper, longer, and winding staircase to the top. When they reached the top, they all gasped; the view was breath-taking. They could see the whole city.

"It's beautiful," said Trashcat.

"It really is," Stinkmutt agreed.

"We have been up here many times, and it always looks more spectacular every time," said Olivia.

"Wow," said Snowy.

They stayed up there for a few more minutes then headed down.

Chapter Six: The Brooklyn Bridge

The next day they got on the ferry and rode back to land, and then walked around for a little while. Then Stinkmutt saw a very big bridge

"Hey," said Stinkmutt. "Do you see that big bridge?"

"Yeah," said Snowy.

They walked down the street to the bridge. Stinkmutt saw a sign pointing to the bridge; it said THE BROOKLYN BRIDGE.

"Hey," said Stinkmutt. "That bridge is called the 'Brook-leen' Bridge."

"It is pronounced 'Brooklin,'" said Olivia.

"Oh yeah. But then why does it have a 'y' in it?"

"The English language is crazy," Olivia said.

They walked down the street a little bit farther and up on the bridge.

"I wonder why there are so many bike locks on the bridge," said Stinkmutt.

"They are called love locks," Olivia explained. "If someone is in love, they will put a lock on the bridge." Then they walked across the bridge.

Chapter Seven: The Dogcatcher's Revenge

When they reached the other side of the bridge, they saw a sign that said, "You are now entering Brooklyn."

"So we are in a different city?" asked Stinkmutt.

"No," said Snowy. "We are just in a different part of New York. The city is broken up into five parts: Manhattan, Brooklyn, The Bronx, Queens, and Staten Island. The parts are called boroughs."

"Wow," said Stinkmutt.

"Oh, no," said Snowy.

"What?" asked Olivia.

"It's Tom!" Tom the dogcatcher was running down the street towards them, but this time he had five other dogcatchers with him.

"Run!" yelled Stinkmutt. They ran and ran. Then they came to a bridge with some empty trashcans under it.

"Let's hide in those trashcans!" said Trashcat. They hid in the trashcans. Thankfully the dogcatchers had not seen them hide and ran past. They stayed in the trashcans for a few minutes to make sure they were safe and then climbed out.

"You know," said Trashcat, "I am getting kind of tired of New York."

"Where should we go next?" asked Stinkmutt.

"I know," said Trashcat, "Let's go to Oregon."

The Camping Trip

By Monroe Colbath

Elmira Elementary School

Austin sat with his headphones in and his face in his phone. Suddenly, his little sister Celest ripped his headphones out of his ears.

"Whatchu watchin'?" she asked.

"None of your business!" Austin rolled his eyes.

"Mom wants to see us in the kitchen."

"Oh, no!" Austin thought. "Was this about all the stuff I bought online with my mom's credit card?"

Austin gulped and reluctantly followed his little sister into the kitchen.

In the kitchen, their mom and dad stood next to each other near the counter. They were both smiling and that made Austin less worried. Even though he had taken precautions to make sure that his parents never found out what he bought, Austin knew there was still a chance that they learned how to use the internet.

"So, your Dad and I have been talking. We think it's best that we all have a little time away from technology," their mom explained.

"Mom, we really don't need that!" Austin protested.

"When's the last time you've picked up a book, Austin?" his dad asked. Austin paused.

"A what?"

"Exactly," his father sighed.

Celest and Jayla stared blankly at their brother. How

could one boy be so dumb?

"Anyway kids. WE ARE . . . GOING CAMPING!!!" Austin's mom yelled enthusiastically. She did jazz hands and danced around the kitchen.

Celest and Dad joined in dancing and yelling, "HOORAY!"

Austin sulked onto the floor and started sobbing.

The kid's mother and father started explaining that they were going camping in a place with no Wi-Fi for a week, and that there was a beautiful waterfall near their destination.

Suddenly Austin's only brain cell started to work and he remembered he had mobile data on his phone.

Austin had a habit of looking at the ceiling when he pictured things in his mind. His face lit up with goofy grin as he imagined all the likes he would get on social media. Pictures of camping trips were popular and got lots of likes.

His older sister Jayla interrupted his train of thought.

"Why do you have that stupid grin on your face? And why are you staring at the ceiling? Gosh, how did I get such a dumb brother?"

"I'm just thinking about all the likes I will get on social media when I post pictures of our trip!"

"Mom said we can't bring our phones. That was the point of the trip. No phones! You're such an idiot!" Jayla smirked. She got joy from ruining Austin's day.

Austin sulked to the floor again. His life was surely ruined.

Two days later, Austin was shoved in a cramped car in between his fifteen-year-old sister Jayla, who was sleeping, and his five-year-old sister Celest, who was reading a book.

"What are you doing?" sneered Austin.

"Reading a book," Celest replied.

"What's a book?" Austin said, completely clueless.

"You truly are hopeless big brother, you know that?" Celest

sighed.

"Hey! If you don't have anything nice to say, then don't say it!" their mom scolded from the front seat of the car. Austin cringed.

"Sorry," Celest sighed.

Some time passed. Austin sat there and counted the zits on Jayla's face. He counted ten. Then he counted all the freckles on Celest's face. He came up with about one hundred and twenty. Then he counted all the chips in the chip bag that his mom brought as a snack. But soon, counting pointless things got boring.

Austin sat there and contemplated his existence. How many stars were in the sky? Is the universe infinite? What is life?

"Hey, Jayla!" Austin muttered.

"What do you want?" Jayla replied rudely.

"If you spill cleaning products, do you make a mess?" Austin asked, sounding as if he was lost in thought.

"I don't know! Why would I know?" Jayla growled.

"Hey, Jayla?" Austin muttered again.

"What?" Jayla glared.

"If you kill a killer, does the number of killers in the world stay the same?"

"Kill two," Jayla said, blandly.

"Hey, Jayla?"

"WHAT DO YOU WANT?!" By this point Jayla was fed up with her little brother.

"Nothing is on fire, fire is on things."

Jayla face palmed.

"Jayla, I'm gonna test your intelligence. If you have three apples and your friend asks for two, how many apples do you have?"

"Three," Jayla muttered

"Your friend forces you to give them the apples, now how many do you have?"

"Three apples and a corpse."

"Mom! Are we almost there?" Celest asked about five minutes later.

"No, it'll be three more hours or so in the car," replied their father.

To pass the time, Austin decided to kick Jayla to see how many kicks it would take to annoy her. Then he repeated the process with his sister Celest. It took twenty-seven to annoy Celest, and it took one to annoy Jayla.

"How much longer?" Austin asked, sure that lots of time had passed.

"About two hours and forty-five minutes," Austin's dad said.

Austin thought he might go insane. There was no way on the planet that only fifteen minutes had passed.

"I need to get OUT of this car and go back to my video games!" Austin thought.

Austin sat there and closed his eyes. He tried with all his might to get his brain to come up with a plan. It didn't have to be a good plan, it just needed to be a plan. If he didn't come up with one soon, he might DIE!

At that moment, Austin remembered a show he watched called *Kirby*. It was about a girl who had a radioactive hedgehog named Kirby that could fly, and the government was trying to hunt them down. Anyway, in the show, the girl—Kathy—got kidnapped and was being taken to the president in a car. She told the FBI agent who was taking her that she had to pee, and instead she bolted away and escaped. Boom, Austin had his plan.

"MOM, I HAVE TO PEE!" Austin yelled.

"Ok, let's stop on the side of the road," his mom suggested.

"NO!" Austin said. "When is the nearest gas station?"

"Ten minutes. Can you wait?" asked Austin's dad.

Austin looked at his sister Jayla. He gave her the look that siblings give each other to say "It's about to go down."

At the gas station, Austin insisted he go in alone. He was happy when he saw that the window in his stall led out to the back parking lot by a huge forest. All Austin had to do was step onto the toilet seat, lift up the window, shimmy his way out, bolt into the forest, and somehow find his way home. Easy as cake, right?

Austin made one fatal mistake, he didn't close the lid of the toilet, and he slipped and fell into the gross toilet bowl.

"Darn diddly darn it!" Austin cried. He made a second attempt and grasped at the window sill. It was too high for him to reach, even on the toilet seat.

The third time's the charm. Austin took a leap and grabbed the windowsill with one arm. His foot dangled into the toilet water, but he didn't care. Quickly he swung his left arm up to grab the windowsill. He pulled himself up a little just so his fingers touched the clip that opened the window.

Austin was panting, it was exhausting! He wished he hadn't skipped doing pull ups and sit ups in P.E.

Austin messed with the clip for a while before he heard noises outside the bathroom. It sounded like his dad. In one swift movement Austin let go of the window sill with his right arm and pushed himself up with his left arm. He reached the clip, unclipped it, and shoved the window up. Using the last of his strength, he shoved the upper half of his body out the window, and at that moment his dad entered the bathroom.

"Austin, are you there?" he asked.

Austin tried to get himself out of the window, but he was stuck. Darn all those chips he ate on the drive!

Feeling defeated Austin called, "Hey, Dad, I'm in here. And I'm stuck."

"What do you mean?" his dad asked.

"I'm stuck in the window. I can't unlock the stall door. I think you need to call someone."

Austin's dad got under the stall door and unlocked it. He stood in awe at his son, who was halfway out of a small window in a bathroom stall.

"How did you . . . ?" he asked under his breath.

"Please don't ask, Dad."

Austin's mom called the fire department, which was thirty minutes away, so Austin was gonna be stuck for a while longer.

Jayla was surprised that they didn't hang up when their mom said, "My son is stuck in a window in a bathroom stall."

The fire department arrived. They sent two men named Frank and Jim. Frank was inside talking to Austin, and Celest looked at Jim.

"So, you get a lot of calls like this?" she asked.

"You'd be surprised," Jim sighed.

Frank came out holding Austin like he was a princess who just got rescued from a tower. "I have successfully rescued the child from the bathroom stall, but how did he get there?"

"Well . . . it's a long story," Austin sighed. "By the way, can you please put me down?"

After telling his parents and the firefighters the very long story, and watching his mother's expression change from angry to furious, he also noticed how the firefighters were obviously holding in laughter.

"Well, Ma'am, I have to say this is the strangest call we have ever gotten. And one woman called us because her pet koala got stuck in a tree. Her pet KOALA!" Jim exclaimed.

"Koalas are supposed to be in trees," Jayla murmured.

"Exactly," Frank told her. "Now that I think of it, we have never been called because of an actual fire."

The two firefighters got in their truck and drove away.

The family's trip was ruined. They didn't continue their trip, they just went home, and Austin was scolded on the drive, but not punished.

When he got home, Austin opened up the local newspaper. He was on the front page!

Austin was so proud of himself! He decided to post a picture of the newspaper on social media. In the end, I guess the camping trip didn't help anyway.

Disappearing Act

By Emily Krauss

Pleasant Hill Middle School

"I think I caught something."

These were the famous last words of Josh Williams, a well-known fisherman who was running his live TV show off the coast of the Bahamas, when the cameras cut and he was never heard from again. His boat was found wrecked nearby and that was the end of it. Oh, and Josh Williams was my father.

That was fifteen years ago, and today whilst on vacation in the Bahamas, I see him. It's from across the street though, and the streets are thick with tourists, so he is gone by the time I get there.

He's changed a lot in the past fifteen years, but it was him. His hair has grown out of its cropped style and now reaches down to his shoulders in a shaggy style. His clean-shaven face now has a mussy beard on it. His right arm and left leg are decorated with webs of tattoos. His legs and arms are more muscular, and he has many scars covering his body. However, I would know this man anywhere. The man who raised me until I was twelve. The man I grew up respecting. The man who was my idol.

If he's alive, then that raises a much more concerning realization. I don't have a dead father. I have a father who didn't care enough to stick around. A father who didn't love me enough to be there for me. And that is a horrible thing to imagine.

It's his fault. His fault I spent six years with my neglectful aunt after my mother died. I rub my chest as I feel all the pent up anger and angst start to writhe around in my heart. I take a deep breath and make a silent vow to myself to find him and make him pay for what he did to me.

I look out of my hotel window and stare into the dark city below. Somewhere out there, my father is sitting in his new house, probably eating dinner, maybe even with a new family. The thought . . . horrifying.

I hardly sleep, and in the morning I set out to put my plan into motion. I first draw up some plans, but they are all too time-consuming, so I grab my bag and head out into the city and wander around looking for him.

It's a slow process because I have no idea where the heck he is. But, I know that he's got to be somewhere. Hiding, like the coward that he is. I contemplate showing pictures of him to people, asking if they've seen him, then I realize that he looks a lot different . . . this might just be a wild goose chase after all.

Walking down the streets in Nassau, Bahamas is supposed to be a relaxing vacation away from reality; instead, it has opened up another whole door of stress and anxiety for me. So . . . fun vacation, am I right?

Anyway, I know that he's out there just waiting for me to find him. The whole day goes by without me finding him. I come home at one o'clock in the morning tired and defeated. The only hope I have is that the next search will be more fruitful.

I wake up and take a nice relaxing hot shower. I put on jean shorts and a tank top and tennis shoes with thick soles before I head out to grab a quick bite to eat. The weather outside is hot and humid, and the streets are crowded with people. I look around, but it's impossible to see anything through the thick smog of people.

I feel myself starting to freeze up and quickly duck into an alley where I can rest and catch my ragged quick breath. Just as I do, my phone starts ringing, I look and see it's Jake. I'm just not in the mood, so I take a deep breath and put the phone back into my backpack. As I put my back against the wall and take a deep breath, thinking about how much my life has fallen apart in the past couple of days, a young woman comes bursting out of the crowd into the alley gasping and looking behind her. She doesn't see me for a minute, and when she does, she yelps and jumps backward in surprise.

"Sorry," she said in surprise. "I didn't know that someone else was hiding from the crowd here."

"It's fine," I say, moving forward to introduce myself. "My name is Zariah."

"I'm Ivana," she replies, taking a step back and putting her hands on her hips.

Ivana has a very tan complexion and is wearing running shorts with a loose-fitting tee shirt. She has very muscular arms and legs, and two blue studs in each ear with a gold locket hanging around her neck. Her dark chocolatey brown hair hangs down around her shoulders in perfect ringlets. Her eyes are a dark brown that seem to be studying me with such intensity that it is almost scary.

"What are you doing here?" she asks skeptically, as if she thinks I am some dangerous criminal.

"I'm on vacation." I almost tell her about my dad, but then decide that I don't know her well enough to tell her that.

"I live here," she tells me almost haughtily.

I choose to ignore her and ask, "Do you ever get used to the crowds around here?"

She sighs and looks around. "I guess not. I've lived here my whole life, and I can barely stand to be around one of those crowds for more than ten minutes."

I look around towards the back of the alley and see a way to a back street that seems semi-empty. I motion for her to go first, and then follow. As we're walking, we pick up some small talk. I don't know why we both don't just keep our heads down and keep walking. But call it what you want, fate or destiny, we keep walking together and don't stop talking . . . or walking. We just keep going. And we walk like that for the whole day. At the end of the day, she gives me her number and I get back to my hotel, trying to ignore the nagging feeling in the back of my head that tells me that I got nothing done today, except find another person who could walk out of my life.

I get up in the morning, feeling the heavy weight of disappointment settle on my back, hunching me over, weighing heavily on me. I walk over to the sink and look in the mirror, at my waist-length wavy brown hair. My bright blue eyes contrast heavily with my deep tan and dark hair. I have naturally long lashes that seem to frame my eyes perfectly. I don't mean to brag, but by most people's standards, I'm very pretty. I look in the mirror for one last second before throwing on a pink tank top and jean shorts. I look down at my phone and surprisingly see five missed calls. They're all from Ivana. I look at my messages and see that she wants to meet me at a popular food place in town. I sigh and reply with a simple but nonchalant *sure*. I stuff my phone in my backpack, open the door of the hotel, and walk out in the streets taking a deep breath, inhaling the street food and the smell of the seawater off to my far right.

I step forward onto the street and immediately almost get

hit by a bike that's riding by. I jump back as the bike hurdles forward and take that as a bad omen for my day.

The cafe is not far away, so I decide to walk. I am definitely not chancing that snail-paced traffic. When I get to the cafe, it's a small place. The front is a baby blue and pink with a nice sign, very cute and rustic. I open the door and a small bell rings. The lady from the counter looks up at me from her phone and gives me a phony smile. She looks right back down on her phone and continues scrolling on it. I sigh and take a seat and take out my own phone to see if Ivana texted me. She hasn't. I scroll through Insta while I wait for her. This time is different though. This time, instead of checking out what my friends are doing, I scour through my dad's old friends' pages trying desperately to come up with anything. Nothing.

Pretty soon, Ivana comes in—out of breath, but cheerful. She smiles at me and then says, "Sorry, I didn't mean to be late, but my parents were really concerned about where we were going. Like I haven't been to this coffee shop a million times, but whatever."

I smile back and invite her to take a seat. "So," I say, taking a deep breath, inhaling the sweet yet bitter smell of coffee as it wafts through the air. "What do you want to do today?"

"First I want to get a nice hot cappuccino, and then we can walk around the city for a little while see the sights," she says getting up to go get coffee. "Do you want anything?"

"Sure, large house coffee black, no sugar or cream," I tell her, looking back down at my phone out of habit.

She gets the coffee and then sits down and we talk for about an hour. We walk around, all whilst I'm looking for him. I don't even know what to call him anymore. He doesn't deserve "Dad" or any form of that. His name is probably not Josh anymore and "HEY YOU!" seems really weird. Well, I guess that we can cross that bridge when we get there.

We're walking around when the mid-day heat really gets to me. It's about 100 degrees outside and super humid. I stumble, and almost fall as I feel myself becoming increasingly faint. Ivana catches me on my way down and then the world seems to fade out slowly, like a bad black and white film.

I come to, and I'm inside some random building that has low ceilings with lights on the ceiling that seem almost blinding. I move in the chair and try to swallow, but feel the dryness in my mouth and I can't swallow. My mouth is almost sticky and my limbs feel heavy. I move my head to the side. It's a struggle, but I manage. I feel the movement of the cold compress on my forehead as I move my head. I see Ivana standing at the counter with a pretty woman who has light brown hair and a curvy figure.

They are standing next to each other talking in hushed tones. I open my mouth to speak and instead hear a sound not different from one a mouse makes. They both look over at me and then slowly walk over. I yawn and then ask in a hoarse whisper that is the only sound I can make, "What happened?"

The blond woman speaks up. "You had a minor heat-stroke."

I sit up and look around confused. "Why am I not at the hospital?"

Ivana looks up from the ground and says, "This is my mama. She is a doctor at the nearby hospital—"

"And I didn't think that you needed to be admitted to the hospital," the lady interrupts.

"Well, thanks for saving me," I say, moving my leaden tongue around in my mouth.

"Yeah," Ivana said, "And I'm so glad that you get to meet my family."

"Yeah, me, too," I tell her as her mother starts walking back to the kitchen.

"Want to stay and have dinner with us?" her mom asks whilst mixing something in a bowl. A smell of something good wafts over from the kitchen and makes my hunger pangs go crazy, like a pack of rabid dogs.

"Yes, please," I say, licking my lips in anticipation.

Ivana hands me a glass of water, and I take a huge gulp, right as the door opens.

He walks in. Yes, my father walks in with a hippy gross man-purse slung over his shoulder. I then proceed to spit the water all over Ivana. When he sees me, he drops the phone he's holding and his jaw hits the floor.

During this whole interaction, Ivana and her mom just stand there, clueless. "Zariah?" he asks as he steps forward in amazement.

"Yes?" I say taking a step away from him.

"What are you doing here?" he asks me in a quiet voice.

"No, the better question is what are YOU doing here?" I ask in a dangerous tone.

He looks at the ground and rubs his forehead. "I guess I owe you an explanation, don't I," he says softly.

"Owe her an explanation for what, Dad?" Ivana asked him urgently, and that one word blows me back a couple of steps. Dad. How is that fair that she got to grow up with a dad, one who was always there for her, while I had to be stuck by myself, bouncing from relative to relative, and then from foster home to foster home?

"She's . . ." he says. "She's my niece."

Rising from the Ashes

The Fading Friend

By Emma Martins

Willamette High School

My brother Eli had just turned seven when he split his head open. My family and I were hiking when he tripped and fell. He got fourteen stitches and had to stay at the hospital for a while. Visiting him is the earliest memory I have. Just the two of us, our smiling faces looking down at all the toys and cards he'd been sent. We played for hours, all the way until we fell asleep.

Since then, it was as if I never left his side. As well as brothers, we were also best friends. I didn't seem to have any memories that he wasn't a part of. Anywhere from school to doing homework or from playing at the park to camping, we always did everything together. Just him and me, Eli and Brody against the world.

Three days after Eli's ninth birthday, the sky was particularly bright while the sun warmed us up just right. This meant there were loads of new presents to use, and today was just the perfect day to do that.

"Hurry up, Brody! We've got lots to do. We can't chance another perfect day like this!" said Eli. I had just thrown on my shoes as he was walking out the door.

"Wait! You've got to tell Mom and Dad that we're going

outside," I said. The last time we forgot, they had not been too happy with us. Realizing his mistake, he came back inside and practically ran to them.

"Mom! Dad! Can Brody and I go outside? We've got lots of new presents to use, and I promise that we'll stay off the streets!"

Rather than reply, they just looked at each other, seeming sad or maybe concerned. They looked like this more often now, but I just couldn't figure out why. I wanted to ask, but something always stopped me.

"Honey, about that. We actually wanted to talk to you," Mom said.

Eli, looking startled, said, "Oh, are all my presents all right?"

"Yes, your presents are fine," replied Dad, "But why don't you come sit down?"

Rather nervous, we both began to walk over when Eli stopped and turned to me, "They only said me. You can go and start playing if you want."

"Oh, ok" I said. As I was turning to leave, I could see that look again on our parents faces. I just hoped nothing was too wrong.

I don't remember much of what happened the rest of that day. It all passed by like a blur. It was like that for the whole week. Maybe I was getting sick. I had probably gotten it from Eli. He seemed to be down the whole week, too.

We spent most of our time at the park. One night, we had gotten home and were getting ready for bed when I mentioned a movie we both wanted to see. It was going to come out the next Wednesday, and we always liked to watch movies on opening day. As soon as I mentioned the date, he changed again, his eyes losing that curious sparkle and his shoulders slumping. It dawned on me that he hadn't been sick that week, he was just sad.

"You've been acting down this whole week. Are you all right?" I asked him. It was weird to see him sad like that.

As he climbed into his bed, he looked at me for a second, hesitating, and then finally saying, "Do you remember last week when Mom and Dad wanted to talk to me?"

"Yeah," I replied. "What had they wanted to talk to you about?"

"They . . . they said that they think I might have a problem in my brain."

My heart dropped. I couldn't let anything happen to him. He's my little brother and my best friend. There wasn't a day I remember spending without him.

"Well, what kind of problem?" I asked. The faster I knew, the faster I could help him.

"They said that I'm seeing things," he merely whispered. "They want me to see a doctor."

Silence. For a while that's all there was. To be quite honest, I was worried. Maybe when he had hit his head back then, it caused long-term effects. How did I not notice? I was with him every day. I must be a horrible brother.

After a few minutes, Eli finally said, "The appointment is on Wednesday. That's when they want me to see the doctor."

"Listen Eli, I just want you to get better, and if Mom and Dad think you should see a doctor, then it's probably the right thing to do," I said. "But just remember, I'll always be there to make you happy again. I don't want to see you down like this."

Resting his hand on the switch, Eli looked at me with a sad smile, saying thank you as he turned off the light.

It had been a month since that day when Eli and I played at the park. He'd had two appointments since then. As the days went on, I felt worse than ever. I could barely remember anything of the last month, and I'd become very pale. I usually pushed these thoughts away when I was with Eli. He seemed to be getting better. He was more cheery and had even told me of new friends he'd made.

Yet today was different, and I decided to let him know about me being sick. When I told him, his shoulders immediately slumped and his eyes drooped.

"About that. You've never been to one of my appointments, and the doctor said it's actually best if you come with me on my last one today."

As we drove to the doctors, Eli didn't say much, he just glanced at me from time to time. I felt worse than ever but put on a happy face for him, as if nothing was wrong. I stared at my hands, noticing that as we got closer, they seemed to be getting more and more pale, almost to the point of being transparent.

By the time we were all sitting down in her office, I could almost completely see through them.

"Hi, Eli. Do you remember what we talked about last week?" the doctor asked. He nodded sadly.

Turning to address Mom and Dad, she said, "Remember, it's important that he does this last part on his own," leading them out of the room.

I turned to Eli. "What's happening?"

"Remember how I said I was seeing things?"

"Yeah, you never actually told me what you were seeing," I replied.

Eli looked at me and I noticed a tear running down his cheek, "I was seeing you."

"Huh? Of course you can see me. I'm real," I said cautiously. Maybe the problem was worse than just seeing things.

"Remember when I had just turned seven and we'd all gone hiking?" he asked me.

I nodded.

"Well, I didn't trip. You pushed me out of the way."

Suddenly the memories came flooding back. I was a few yards away from Eli when I noticed he was standing on a ledge that wasn't very stable. With the slow cracking sound that flooded my ears and the very evident cracks that only seemed to be getting bigger, I broke into a sprint. Reaching out for him, I was able to pull him to safety. Unfortunately, during the process, I lost my footing and fell with the very same ledge I had saved him from.

I looked down and realized I was shaking.

"You died that day, Brody, and after all this time, you've just been a figment of my imagination."

"No, but I'm real! I have to be!" I said frantically, my heart beating faster than ever.

"Think of all your memories. Have you ever been by yourself? Been without me?"

I didn't want to believe it because it just couldn't be true, but at the same time it was the only explanation. Every single memory I had was of him. Every decision and action I'd ever made was with him. Every feeling of joy, sadness, frustration, and excitement I'd ever felt was with him.

Looking down at my body once again, I realized that I was no longer skin and bone, but rather a mere outline of a boy.

"I have to go, don't I?" I asked.

He nodded.

What was going to happen to me? The thought of just fading away was the most frightening thing I had ever experienced, but even worse than that was the idea of never being able to see Eli again. Everything in me wanted to tell Eli to forget about what the doctor said and keep me here forever, but my heart said otherwise. Ever since the first day I started feeling sick, Eli continued to get better. He had friends and was really happy, and to me that's all that mattered.

"So I guess this is goodbye then. I've always just been your imaginary friend and brother."

"No, you were real. You just had to leave so soon," he said, looking down, his voice barely audible.

As the door began to open, Eli looked at me and said his last goodbye.

"Don't forget me," I whispered.

Eli gave me one last sad, reassuring look, and with that, I completely began to fade away, forever being remembered in the back of Eli's mind. His imaginary friend and Brother.

Heart of Ice

By Brianna Bird

Eugene Christian School

It was a cold rainy morning that Jack saw her. He had been walking his path to the mill, when he glanced up beneath the window of the master's house. Her skin was white, deathly pale. Her chest rose and fell in shuddering gasps, and her eyes were hollow and empty. She was clearly human, but she was otherworldly, as though from another side of the sky. But she was beautiful. Jack stared, as she slowly turned her eyes toward him. Her hair was dark, and she smiled sadly at him through the window. Though her voice was soft and the rain was fast, Jack could make out the words as though they had been whispered in his head.

"They say I'm not long for this world."

Jack nodded, grimly. "Do you mind it?"

She smiled. "No. I only wish I could have been strong enough to be someone in this life."

Chills ran up the boy's cold form. "I wish I could have married you."

"I know you not, yet the feeling is mutual."

She turned away, and Jack continued along the road, letting the rain wash away the horror of moments ago.

The next day, he saw a stone coffin trekking along the same road. Few mourners trailed behind, an older man, a priest, and another older couple. The rain had doubled. Jack joined a little behind, not caring if he was late for work. The coffin was lowered into a freshly dug grave, the smell of earth seeping out of it. The body of the girl seemed like a stain never to be healed but washed by the rain. Jack wished he could have kissed her deathly pale lips. Jack did not even know her name. He knelt beside the head stone, sinking his trousers into the mud. He sat there for hours, not minding cold, nor hunger. At last, as the dark began to come on, the village boys dragged him to his feet. He went.

"Did you know her?" It was Simon, the oldest boy.

"Briefly."

"Did you love her?"

"Yes."

* * *

Jack's breath was not his own. It was a machine's. Thousands of beeps rang in his ears, the sound of nurses and patients discussing health care issues. Jack was done with that. He didn't have a lot of time before his heart burst out of his chest. He had only one daughter, and she was in Chicago. He had forced her to stay on her honeymoon, insisting it only happened once. Jack's only companion was a small tabby cat, curled upon his chest, snoring. She was only allowed on when the doctors were gone.

Jack looked out the window, praying that it would be the last time he ever did. An older teenage girl, possibly sixteen, balanced on a curb. She looked extremely familiar. The wind was raging, but her hair, however, was not stirring. She leapt onto the brick ledge, and soon she was scaling the wall. Jack, too startled to respond, simply stared. She was immensely familiar, and there was something not quite right about her. For one, no one in the crowded courtyard below seemed to notice her, except Jack. The closer she got, the more he noticed odd things about her. Her chest did not expand and deflate like it should have, and her eyes stayed wide open at all times, never blinking. She was so familiar. He also had not realized the window could open. It rather surprised him when it did, and the girl, looking very sure of herself, stepped in. She walked toward him, coming to stop beside his bed.

"Hello, Jack. Are you ready? I'm sorry, but you'll have to leave Storm here."

Jack looked at her, stunned. "How do you know her name?"

She laughed. "Don't you recognize me?"

Jack nodded, confused. "Yes, although I don't know from where."

"Let's just say I'm not long for this world."

"So, this is what's become of you then?"

"Raptured, you mean, yes. Are you coming?" She reached out her hand to the man.

It was beautiful, but healthy, like he remembered it. Slowly, he took it, and suddenly he was standing outside the window, butterflies flying around him. Storm was sitting up on the man's body, pawing his face. Jack looked away, gripping the girl's hand. He was surprised to see that he was six feet tall again, and that he had dark brown hair, green eyes, and a daring eighteen-year-old smile. He stepped forward, and soon he was gliding forward across clouds and rivers. He looked over at the girl, suddenly knowing her name was Rebbeckah. She looked at him, tears in her glowing eyes. She threw her arms round his neck and whispered two words, "Welcome home."

Skyline

By Natasha Dracobly

South Eugene High School

"I think friends are better than dating," Sandy told me once, back in fifth grade. We barely knew what the difference was then, but it didn't stop us having opinions. "Who likes boys anyways?"

"Boys are gross," I said. I was always eager to tag onto her thoughts, hanging on her nods of approval when I said the right thing. I just wanted her to like me, in whatever way I needed to.

I didn't really know why. Sandy wasn't interested in drawing or in science, which were normally the only things I cared about, but she drew me to her all the same. I thought she could do no wrong. The first time I heard her say something, when a teacher chose her to read a poem for our fourth grade class, I made up my mind to become friends with her. It wasn't a long poem, just a few lines about spring and flowers or something, but the way she moved her hands as she spoke struck me like sunlight in a crack between clouds, and the lilt of her voice sounded how I thought the stars should. I went up to her at recess that day and asked if she wanted to be friends. I spent the next six years worrying she'd change her mind.

"We won't ever get boyfriends," she declared that day in fifth grade, and flipped her dark hair over one shoulder. I loved that hair. "We're going to hang out with each other." Of course, I agreed.

* * *

The remnants of August linger in the hot air as I sit on the porch swing, despite the fact that it's now definitely September. I check my texts again, probably the third time in the last five minutes. The only thing that appears is one from my aunt, telling me how my cousin won his soccer game. I ignore it. I'm only looking at my conversation with Sandy.

I haven't seen Sandy in three months now, the longest period since we first met. This summer her grandfather got really sick, and the whole family's been in Japan since June caring for him. They're only coming back now because school's starting up again. Beginning of sophomore year in a few days. Sandy and I have a tradition for the last weekend before school starts. We have a sleepover, just the two of us, and stay up all night watching movies and talking, like a last hurrah before we have to schedule our lives once again.

While I wait, I scroll through our old conversations, trying not to feel nervous. It's not like Sandy and I haven't seen each other's faces recently — we FaceTime whenever we can. I know she's dyed her hair pink at the tips, and started wearing winged eyeliner. I know she still makes the same jokes as she did three months ago.

But my stomach still fills with butterflies when I see her mom's minivan come around the corner and park in front of our house. My fingers feel sweaty, and I put my phone in my pocket to ensure I don't drop it when I see Sandy.

I stand up, starting to walk down the steps to the sidewalk. It takes seven steps exactly to get there. I've counted it a million times. The car door opens and Sandy steps out. Her hair looks more pink than it did on FaceTime. The backpack she's carrying looks new. I wave, and she waves too, grinning. Her smile is even prettier than I remember.

I count my steps and hers, one, two, three, and then we're standing right in front of each other, only one step apart. If our paths were crossing in a parallel universe, maybe I would kiss her now.

As it is, she hugs me instead. Sandy smells like lavender. She's worn that perfume since her grandma gave it to her in eighth grade. It's my favorite scent, though I've never loved lavender.

"I missed you," I say when she releases me. I want to tell her many things about this summer, like the loneliness and the achiness of my heart and the three sketchbooks I filled mostly with drawings of her with the cherry-blossom trees. I don't say anything more.

Sandy bites her lip and grabs my hand, pulling me around and inside. My heart speeds up to twice as fast, but I know she doesn't mean anything of it. "I missed you, too. Let's go in! I need to say hi to your mom, you know."

"I know." I tell myself I'll talk to Sandy about it later, but I know I won't. I've been not saying it for almost four years.

My mom's already at the door when we walk in, and Sandy greets her with the same hug she gave me. Sandy's spent so much time here over the years that she's practically part of the family.

"I already ordered the pizza," she says, and Sandy somehow smiles even wider. She smiles a lot.

"Sandy and I are going upstairs. Call us when the pizza gets here?"

My mom nods and shoos us away. "Of course. Have fun!"

* * *

"How was Japan?"

The light is fading now from the sky, leaving only the darkest blue against the trees. If I looked carefully, I'd see stars starting to appear. This used to be Sandy's favorite time of night, I know, but she told me that three years ago, and I know she's changed since then.

We're not in our pajamas yet, and seeing her hand next to mine on the bed, I can't help but notice how different we seem. She looks pretty and put together and well groomed, with perfectly manicured pink nails matching her dyed pink hair. I'm wearing some sweatpants I found in my closet today, and I don't think I've done my nails in years.

"It was nice, mostly," she says. "Different from here though. I wish you could have seen it."

"I wish I could have, too," I say. I don't trust myself to say anything more than that.

She takes my hand and squeezes it in hers. "Someday we should go together."

My face feels hot at that comment. I imagine being in Japan with Sandy, just the two of us. I imagine going to museums with her and taking selfies in front of statues, and staying in a hotel together, and planning where we'd go next. I imagine kissing her there, too, but I shake my head and wave those fantasies away.

"We'll need money for that."

Sandy laughs. "You need money for everything, idiot! We'll have jobs then, anyway."

"I know that." I wonder what kinds of things Sandy wants to do. I wonder why I still don't know. I used to think I knew everything about Sandy. It kind of scares me now, as I realize that's not true. "What kinds of jobs do you think you want?"

"I don't know. I'm not sure how everyone expects us to have it all figured out already." She pauses, looks down at where our hands sit on the bed, still together, and smiles. Like an idiot, I hope she's smiling at that, but then she looks up again. "I mean, when I was five I had it all figured out."

I shake my head. "What?"

"I was going to be an astronaut. And a princess, too. I made my parents dress me up as a space princess for Halloween that year."

"That's amazing."

"They thought so, too."

She blinks. Her winged eyeliner makes her dark eyes look even prettier. I really need to stop.

"Do you still like space much?"

I only get a shrug at that. "I haven't thought about it in years. I think I'd still like the stars."

"I think the stars are the best thing in the world," I say.

She nods. "Do you remember in sixth grade, when we climbed on your roof to look at the stars? That was fun."

"We could do it again, you know. The roof's still up there."

She laughs, and I laugh in return, but it fades. I feel awkward now, in a state between our easy friendship before, when we always understood what the other was thinking, and something lesser. I feel like something's broken, not that I want to think it. The thought nearly breaks my heart.

"Do you want to?"

"Sure." I stand up, tugging on her hand to pull her up with me. She helps me open the window and then we climb out, me in front of Sandy, helping her through.

The roof is slightly slanted, but we stand on it without fear, stretching our hands up to feel the wind. The sky is almost pitch black, and the moon is nowhere to be seen. There are only the stars with us now.

* * *

"If the world was new today, what would you do?"

Sandy lies next to me on the roof. The pink tips of her long hair fly with the wind. When she looks up, her face is a perfect silhouette. If I didn't know she'd think it was weird, I'd ask her right now to wait while I grabbed my sketchbook, and then I'd draw her here, with the stars as her backdrop.

"I don't understand," I say. "What do you mean?"

She shrugs, smiles, pursing her lips the way she always does. "Whatever you want it to mean. It's flexible."

"I'm not."

"Not what? Flexible?"

I shrug. "Yeah."

"Then if the world was new to you, what would you do?"

I smile. "To me? I'd be pretty confused then, I think."

Scooting closer to me on the roof, Sandy's foot touches mine. She elbows me. "Go on, think of something."

When my brother elbows me, it's to annoy me, but when Sandy does it, I don't mind at all. I elbow her back, and she finally turns her head away from the stars and smiles at me. I don't think I'll ever get tired of seeing Sandy smile at me. I don't think I'll ever get tired of seeing her in general, really. She's that pretty.

"I guess I'd look at the sky," I say. "If I'd never seen it before, I would be amazed at the sky."

"You're a nerd," she tells me, and I elbow her again.

* * *

It feels more like fall when the temperature drops later that night, leaving us both shivering where we still lie on the roof. We've been quiet for the last hour or two, just lying next to each other and watching the stars appear one by one. I suddenly realize I have goosebumps along my arms, and I hug them close to myself to try and keep warm. I need a sweater. Sitting up, I see Sandy's looking at me.

"I'm just getting a jacket." She nods, and I pause. "If you're cold I can get you one, too."

She shakes her head. "I'm good."

When I climb back through the window and into my room, it feels like a different world. My room is warm and cozy, with stuff on the floor for school and cello and all the art projects I've started and never finished. In a fantasy book, it's what they'd call the normal world.

I grab a navy blue hoodie from next to the bed, where there's a pile of sweaters and hoodies that I'm too lazy to hang up, and shove it over my head before going back through the window.

Standing on the roof, with the breeze on my face, chilling my nose, the world looks different. The sky is so dark and the stars so bright, and all the lights from the city below can't possibly compare to the beauty of space.

"Hey," Sandy says from below me. I reach for her hand, lying on the roof tiles.

"Look. Isn't it beautiful?"

She takes it, but looks confused. "Yeah. Don't you want to lie down?"

"No." I smile. "Here, stand up." She stands, and then we are together above it all, looking down at the world as we hold hands. Well, she's looking at the world. I'm just looking at her. "Isn't it incredible?"

"I guess it is kind of cool."

"It's really cool."

"Really cool, then," she says.

There's a silence. My drama teacher calls it a beat. In theatre, beats usually only go before particularly important or dramatic lines. They have to be earned. But in real life, beats are often meaningless. They come in whenever we don't have words to say.

"So, did you meet anyone in Japan?" The fingers of my left hand are crossed at my side. I'm trying to keep my smile.

"Meet? Not really."

I nod, try to breathe. "Is there any one you're interested in?"

Sandy shakes her head quickly. "Not right now."

"Oh." We're still holding hands. "That's cool."

"Actually I am interested in someone." Her words are rushed, tumbling out of her mouth. She's not looking at me.

"Who?" I ask. I feel a kind of pit in my stomach. Of course she's interested in someone.

"I don't know, guess. I've been pretty obvious."

I shake my head. I don't think I can breathe. "No, I have no idea."

She sighs, then looks back up at the sky. I look up too, but there's nothing there. Just stars. She sighs again, and I don't think she's going to say anything, but then she turns back to me.

"Can you really not see it?"

I giggle. Try, anyway. It sounds more like a cough. "No, sorry. I'm not very observant."

"You really aren't." She laughs. It sounds bitter, but I don't know why.

"I'm really sorry—"

"It's you, idiot."

"What?" I've heard her wrong. Or understood her wrong. Or something. She can't be interested in me.

"I like you. I have for months. Almost a year now, really."

Her voice is blank. She doesn't look at me.

"You do?" She does?

"Yeah."

I blink, once, twice, three times. "Oh."

"It's fine you don't feel the same way. I'm good with being friends. I don't want you to think we can't just be friends." Her words are moving fast again, and my brain, addled from what she'd just said, can barely keep up.

"And what if I do feel the same way?"

Sandy's head snaps around to look at me. Her eyes stare into mine. "Do you?"

I shrug. "Yeah."

Sandy smiles. We're still holding hands, and she brings me closer to her. She is very close now. I can see the individual strands of her hair. I could count her eyelashes. Sandy is holding me, and despite the slant of the roof, I know I won't fall. I smile, briefly, and then she leans in and kisses me.

The sky watches us kiss. It is dark outside, and there is nothing here but us and the wind and the stars.

Made in the USA
Middletown, DE
25 August 2020